THE STROKE OF LIFE

By Donald Herring

D1502569

Preface

The writing of this book came as a big surprise. There was no notion of putting my experience of my stroke on paper. You see people have strokes all the time and from all walks of life. There is no class of people exempted from this killer. There is no color line. There is no nationality line or country you might be from. Mr. Stroke can and does strike anyone who has the trait of its origin. I've seen many people with the crippling results of Mr. Stroke. It has been most often senior citizens. Children can and do have strokes too so no one is exempt. After my research into the world of Mr. Stroke I found out that he was closer to me than I had ever imagined. Never thought I would be a part of his world. Having a stroke only happens to old people. Right! I was so wrong. It happened to me an athlete all my life. Never dreamed Mr. Stroke was at my doorstep all these years waiting to ring my door bell and come on in. Because of my unique circumstances of being stricken and recovering I decided to put my story in writing for all to benefit. After all I was given a second chance at life. I believe it's my duty to pass the miracle to others to use and prosper from just as I did. I have told my story to a lot of people through my stroke presentations at senior centers and other venues. Many suggested that I write about it so others could receive my miracle also just as I did.

TABLE OF CONTENTS

Chapter 1: The First Stroke

It was a normal day on the job on Tuesday February 15th 2011 as an inventory controller at the North Ave facility for the City of Atlanta. The job was a very satisfying position in which I worked pretty much alone. I answered only to one person: Mrs. Bishop, a very pleasant lady who tried to act stern but was really a pussy cat. She was a slow meticulous woman but sweet and never micromanaged my work. The purchase of all vehicles, machinery, tools and supplies used to maintain the streets of Atlanta from that city yard were under her department. Whenever you were in her office you would see stacks of papers all over her desk. Every stack had a rhyme and reason for being there. When you entered her office and sat down you would have to sit in the right spot or she would tell you were sitting in the wrong chair and you would have to move to the right spot where she wanted you to sit. If you didn't want to move to the spot she wanted you to a sit she would ask you to leave her office. Why she did this I'll never know, but she did. If you didn't follow her lead in her office you didn't stay. Her office was so nice and quiet though, probably because no one wanted to go through the chair thing. I worked with three other women, Big B, Sweet Dean and Preacher Steph. Big B's name was Bernadette, a very nice lady with some size on her. She wasn't fat, but big boned and tall and had good work ethic. Although she very thorough she was very, very slow. I would ask her to look up some things for me and it would take forever for me to get it back. So I stopped asking her for anything.

My other officemate was Richdean. Now she was miss hippy dippy with big hips, always wearing tight fitting pants. According to her, Mrs. Richdean was on top of all things. Now what it was she was on top of I never knew. As long as I worked in that office with her I never knew what Richdean did. I never saw her talking to anybody on the phone about business. I would see and hear her on the phone but it would never be about city business. It's funny I never saw her do any work, but always talking to someone in the office or on the phone. She had the latest info about any and everything that went on in that City Yard. Although I never saw her do any work she was always sweet. Then there was Stephany. She worked inventory with me making orders of supplies and parts needed for office inventory and special jobs. She had a church Scripture for every message she sent you by cell phone. She would send them to my phone all the time, thus the name Preacher Steph. She was nice and very sweet too. I had never worked with all women before. I've had many positions working in business offices with men and women but never all women. It was very nice though because of the treatment I was given with these ladies. We all worked well together and when the time came we knew when one of us needed to be alone in our own space. It was a good place to work, because everybody's space was respected by all. No fuss no muss atmosphere.

Like most Mondays after work I would go to the gym and work out with weights or go to the boxing gym and hit the bags or spar with the guys a few rounds. Because Monday was Valentine's Day I went to the gym on Tuesday. This is when my first stroke occurred after I arrived home after work that Tuesday. I was so surprised that this happened because I thought my health was so in tip top condition. To understand my thinking you need to know my athletic background.

To give a little history of my athletics I started swimming at three years old. I was diving and jumping off the three-meter board shortly after I learned to swim. My family moved from Los Angeles, California to my father's

9

hometown of Bakersfield shortly after this. We lived in the projects off of California Avenue. Next door to us lived two young guys Alonzo and Elsie. Well Alonzo took an interest in me. Now I don't know if it was because of my mother. You see my mom was a pretty lady and you know how young guys are with pretty mothers with children. Well anyway Alonzo would take me swimming with him on a regular basis. If it wasn't for Alonzo, I wouldn't have learned how to swim so early. At the age of nine I moved back to Los Angeles with my family. I started swimming competitively when I was ten years old at a YMCA in South Central Los Angeles. While in junior high school I started lifting weights and continued swimming until I graduated from high school. While in high school I was a varsity diver; as a matter of fact I was Southern League Champ in summer of 1966. The weight training started at the age of twelve. My five friends and I started at the same time working out with the weights. I became so good they nicknamed me "Muscles." That name stuck with me until I entered high school. To this day my old friends from my neighborhood still call me Muscles even though I am in my sixties. I thought the name was great when we were kids because I was the strongest. As I grew older and left the neighborhood the name seemed to slip away. As I look back I was a small string bean of a little guy. I knew how to make all the muscle poses we saw in the magazines and the guys admired me for that. We all wanted to be bodybuilders. Those times were so much fun. We were so into what we ate at that time we all wanted to be big and strong. I've been into my health ever since.

I've swum on swimming teams and ran track since I was in the sixth grade. Being Southern League swimming champ as a varsity diver at Washington High School in Los Angeles California was big time back in the day. I remember like it was yesterday. I was diving in at a varsity level contest at Los Angeles City High School. I was doing a back dive with no difficulty off the one-meter board. When I made my dive I went straight down into the water without arching my back and hit the bottom of the pool and broke all my front teeth. Now I usually would come to the surface smiling because I always had a winning dive. Well after this dive I didn't come up smiling. I had my hand over my mouth covering my broken teeth much to me and other teammates' surprise. I can still hear the crunch of my teeth on the bottom of that pool after all these years. The depth of the pool wasn't being considered at eight feet by me or my coach when I made the dive because otherwise I would have arched my back and not hit the bottom of the pool. From that day on I never dove in any pool less than ten feet deep. Because of school insurance I was able to get my teeth fixed immediately after the accident. Yes! After the repairs I was able to smile after every dive again in all my swimming meets thereafter. Of course that was a great thing for me as a teenager in high school. I still had a life after swimming every day. After leaving high school I attended Los Angeles Harbor College. I still kept in good shape but didn't swim instead electing to play football which was my dream. My dream was one day to play in the pros. At the time I thought it was a far-fetched dream. It was just a dream unless a miracle happened that I grew a lot larger than I was at 129 pounds. I played football my first year at Harbor College. I didn't get to play much at all unless we were leading by 100 points or so. Now that I look back on it, it was the only thing the coach could do. I was simply too small to play and be effective. I have many great memories at football parties and functions that year though. I remember at a football party my best friend and I were invited as the only Black people. Keep in mind we were invited by my white teammates. So my buddy and I felt we were fine because we were with our team so there shouldn't have been a problem. But to our surprise that just wasn't so.

After some of other people not our teammates got a little buzz from drinking they started getting a little crazy and saying things like "All those who weren't invited please leave." Well my buddy and I looked at each other and said they can't be talking about us because we were invited. About ten minutes later someone said over the loud speaker again. "Those who were not invited please leave." My buddy and I looked at each other again we said "They can't be talking about us because we were invited by our teammates." But as we looked around the room everybody were looking at us. So we looked at some our teammates and they shrugged their shoulders and said "What can we do?" My buddy said "I think they are talking about us." Both doors were blocked so we had to make a decision to stay and fight or leave quietly. We decided to leave quietly because we were outnumbered at the party. Our teammates came up and said "We will all leave too." So we all left the party together. It got kind of scary for a while. My buddy and I didn't know what we were going to do. We were a long way from home with no help if the team hadn't been there for us. Now you know there was not a lot of racial tension at that time in the Los Angeles area during the late 60s, though you might have some bigots here and there like in any city. That was one of many exciting times we had at

Harbor College. I certainly missed those times. Even though I didn't get to play much I was always in great physical shape at all times. I never knew when I was going to get called on to play. All the players on the team would praise me on how good of shape I maintained being such a small guy. My two best friends at Harbor College were Bobby Peters and of course my best friend since junior high school Jerry Haywood. Now I don't know what happen to Bobby when I left Harbor College. I never heard from or saw him again. I only stayed at Harbor College for one year and then went to Los Angeles City College which I only attended for one year also. The only thing I received from LA City College worth remembering is music class with the lead guitarist Tony Maiden for Chaka Khan. We became pretty good friends, but lost touch with each other after I left. We always had some crazy things to talk about in class. I still kept in great shape but didn't participate in any sports at all. I just played the ladies as most young guys did then and attended some classes of no substance because I just didn't know what I wanted do in life. I just didn't. I didn't have any role model who I wanted to emulate as a professional. I was lost there with no idea of what I wanted to be or do. That's a shame for any young person just entering the world of real time business. Unfortunately that's the way it was for me. Now that I am revisiting that time of my life it's scary. I had only my sports dream to hang on to. That's why I continued to keep in shape. My health was so important to me.

After my year at LA City College I attended college at Long Beach State College. While there I took a full load in Business Administration and Political Science classes hoping to find my place in the world. As it was I wasn't able to find my place. I did join the Black Student Union with my high school classmate Dwight Herbert who became Vice President of the BSU at that time. I was elected Sergeant of Arms of the BSU and felt I belonged. I was roommates with the President, Vice President, and Secretary. We had such a wonderful time as officers and roommates. We did so much for the Black student culture on that campus of Long Beach State and across the country on other college campuses also. I can honestly say we made more of a difference in the lives of many Black students who attended colleges all across the nation as part of the Black Student Union which I'm proud to have been a part of during the late 60s. During my stay at Long Beach State College I kept in great shape for my sports ventures like Power Lifting but also Sergeant of Arms of the Black

Student Union. While at Long Beach State I didn't participate in any field sports like track, football but I elected to power lift in the 132-pound class. My health was always a priority even in college. Always staying fit was important to me to enhance the possibility of a long life. With my weightlifting ability I got to be the California Collegiate State Power Lifting Champion in the 132-pound class in 1972. I was fifth in the United State in the 132lb class collegiately. The Collegiate Nationals that year were held in Michigan at Michigan State University (MSU) campus for three days. That was the first time that I ever competed in any college competition out of state representing a major college institution. I stayed on MSU campus in the dorms with other students competing from all across the nation. I went with another student and good friend who also was very good power lifter at Long Beach State at that time. His name was Clifton Marsh. He was in the heavy weight division. I believe he won his division in the collegiate national that year at MSU. He was a monster powerful lifter who was studying to be a professor of literature at Long Beach State. I haven't seen or heard from him since I left Long Beach State, but I think he became a professor at Hampton College later. Clifton was very active in the Black Student Union also. While in Michigan I got to visit Detroit's most famous Watts Mozambique Jazz lounge, where I saw jazz legends The Betty Carter Trio perform. My visit there was one of my most memorable.

That same year I walked on the Los Angeles Rams Training camp of 1972 and got a spot as a running specialist position as a punt and kickoff returner. I was running 4.3 40 yards back to back. I was playing with teammates quarterback John Hadl, TE Jack Snow, WR Harold Jackson, Linemen legions Rosey Grier, Deacon Jones, Merlin Olsen, Lamar Lundy and others from that era. It was a dream come true to play on the same field with these legions. My stay was short (only the preseason) because of my size. That was fine; I knew what my chances were when I walked on. But I was there and that can't be taken away from me. I wish I had taken some photos with my teammates on that LA Rams team. I walked on with a good friend of mine named Eddie Walker. We trained together that whole year before and that summer. Eddie was very fast too. He was much taller than I was 5'10" and he weighed about 185 pounds. So he wasn't a big player but he could run some beautiful pass routes and he was just as fast as I was. They made him a wide receiver and slot back. Head Coach Chuck Knox loved to watch Eddie run his routes. Eddie had excellent hands too. That guy could catch anything that came his way. I mean he was great. Harold Jackson was on one side and Eddie was on the other side. That was a winning combination for the Rams that year. After the preseason I got cut and Eddie went on to play. From there I went to the World League with the Philadelphia Bells in 1973. That only lasted for one year because the league ended the same year.

My health was great during those ball playing years as a running specialist. I made sure my body was in the greatest condition possible to endure those workouts and the pounding of professional football. At this time I thought my body was in the greatest condition ever. I thought nothing could stop me during my professional football career. I was riding high. I was shocked when my career ended with Philly. I was in the best shape of my life. I wasn't doing what I had hoped to be doing for the rest of my young life. What was I going to do? I fell into a deep panic. I was in great health. I wasn't taking any type of health supplements or enhancements. My temple was in excellent working condition. At this time I was thirty years old. What was next? What do I do with myself now? I thought, I'm still young and have so much to do with myself athletically. I can't play professional football anymore. The young guys are bigger, faster and stronger than I am now. What am I going to do with myself? I did some real soul searching. I can't run professional track because I am too short and small. I can't play pro baseball because I am too small and I can't hit the ball along with not being able to catch well either. I can't play pro basketball because I'm too short and I can't shoot worth a damn. What's next? I wondered again.

Chapter 2: Dual Lives

Before I go further into with my background in athletics, I must mention while I was in college I had an interest in chopper motorcycles. So I built myself a chopper motorcycle right before I started attending Long Beach State College. Shortly after building it I joined a Chopper Motorcycle Club in Los Angeles, California at the age of nineteen. Now to be able to handle a 350+pound Chopper motorcycle you must be in shape. You can't be a small winkling. You must be a strong person much less a little person, which I was. I've seen little women with big Harleys so you know I had to own up as a man and get with the program. At that time in Los Angeles there was a women's motorcycle club called Soul Sisters. Now these women were not little prissy women. They were all big stout healthy women. Most of them could and would whip up a man with no problem. Most of the women in the club were lesbians and they would let you know it without any problem. Most could ride better than any man on the street at that time. I mean these women could ride those bikes and look good doing it too. They had beautiful colors that they wore but were a tough group of women in looks and size.

I've never seen any women bike crew look as good as they did since. At that time I was the youngest in the club at nineteen years old. My motorcycle name was (can you believe it?) Baby Chop. The president's name was Mr. Chop. Now in most clubs you have a First Lady who handles all the females in the club and you guessed it—her name was Mama Chop. To this day that is still true in the LA Choppers Motorcycle Club of Los Angeles, California. I still keep in touch with Mr. Chop the president. I still have my colors in the closet ready to wear. Most of the guys that were active when I joined the club have passed on. Even some of the ones that had joined the club after me that were younger than I was are not with us either. That's really something; it makes you think all the things you did while you were young to increase your health were good. While in the club I was a student at Long Beach State College during the week and a bike rider on the weekends.

I had a dual life during that time. While at Cal State Long Beach I was active in the Black Student Union and the Black Panther Party. My roommates were the President Tony Wilkins, Dwight Herbert Vice President, and Warren Haughton Secretary. I remember just like it was yesterday all the sit-ins and student demonstrations we used to participate in trying to get the Black Study programs on that campus for Black students as a major. To be involved in all those activities I had to be in good physical and mental shape to help participate in and put together all the meetings and lectures to convince the powers that be in the California State college schools we as students meant business. We as Black students at that time had a voice in what was studied at our state college schools in California and what we were being taught that we paid taxes for. Today that is nonexistent in any state institutions across the United States. Students have no say in what is taught and what isn't. During our time we Black students would go to jail or fight with our lives on the line for what we believed in. There was pure unity with Black students all across the United States then. Today there is no communication between Black students on college campuses across this nation. Now that I look back on what we did as students then it's frightening that more students weren't killed or injured. Man! We were daring and unafraid at whatever life had to dish out. As I think about it I get chills running through my body. That's something about how we thought about things then. Now those things would not be in any discussions with our youth in today's time.

Getting back to my true athleticism after the World League ended and I left Philadelphia Bells in 73, I didn't know what I was going to do with myself having all this athletic ability. I couldn't run professional track because I was too short and small. I couldn't play professional baseball because I was too small and I couldn't hit. The fact I couldn't catch well either was a problem. I couldn't play professional basketball because I was too short and couldn't shoot well either. So that was out. *Maybe I can box professionally* I thought. I had a friend at Harbor Junior College in Carson California whose father was a professional boxing trainer and Ken Norton's trainer there in Los Angeles at that time. I knew nothing about boxing. I knew only I was in great shape for thirty years old. Now in boxing that is old and a person that old is through in his career in boxing and winding down. He has a championship belt or belts. I was fast on my feet. I could run the 40-yard dash in 4.3 seconds back to back or less. I was strong as a bull at 132 pounds. I had endurance for days. I had no broken bones any place on my body. I was not on any medication of any kind. I was in perfect health. So I said to myself "I can do this". So I set out searching for my friend's dad. I had forgotten my friend's dad's name after eight years with no contact with my friend. So I contacted some friends of mine that knew my friend at Harbor College. I found out his name was Bill Slayton of Boyle Height. I didn't know at the time he was Ken Norton's trainer. He was the type of person to teach anyone who wanted to learn to box if they asked him. He would find the time to fit you in the program. He was that giving of a person with a nice gentle pleasant side. He never raised his voice even when it was something that you did that displeased him. Of course I didn't know all this at the time. So I searched all the most popular gyms in Los Angeles at that time until I found the right one. I went to Main Street Gym on Main Street in the hood, the Hollenbeck Gym in East Los Angeles and I searched the Olympic Gym in Downtown Los Angeles. These were the main gyms for professional fighters at that time. Then I went to the brand new gym called The Broadway Gym. It was in my area where I lived. As a matter of fact it was ten minutes from home. The gym was in its finishing stages at the time. I was so excited when I found the right gym; I didn't know how to control myself. I was so excited about meeting Ken Norton personally and possibly getting to box out of his stable. Just like horses in stables of well-known race horse owners I would be in the stable of a well-known fighter.

When I entered the gym it smelled of new paint and varnish on the wood floors, walls and new boxing equipment all around the gym. As I entered the gym, fighters were jumping rope, hitting heavy bags, speed bags and shadow boxing. It was a real thrill to see all that was going on. As I looked around the gym I saw a familiar face with a muscular body moving around the floor hitting the mitts with a trainer. It was Ken Norton with his trainer my friend's dad Bill Slayton. It was quite exciting to see them go from stage to stage of different workouts: the heavy bag, the mitts, the speed bag, jumping rope and shadow boxing and end up sparing with of course another fighter. It was so exciting it was like watching a Rocky movie and being in it. After the workout was over I went over to Mr. Slayton and Ken to introduce myself. They both were very gracious and pleasant. It was just like I thought it would be with them both being very humble like most well-known athletics are. Anyway I explained who I was and what led me to him. I told him how I knew his son from college and what my intentions were in boxing. I explained my athletic background while he just looked at me up and down with wonder in his smile and delight in his eyes as I talked. He seemed to be impressed to my surprise because I was thirty years old and in great shape. He thought I would be able to endure the rigorous training that would be ahead of me from day one.

During my stay at the Broadway Gym I met some of the best in the sport of boxing: Marvin Hagler, Larry Holmes, Sugar Ray Lenard, Thomas Hearns, Muhammad Ali and others. Mr. Slaton agreed to train me. I stayed with Mr. Slaton from 1973 to 1982 in which I had many fights in southern and northern California and Las Vegas until I left Cali for the East Coast in 1982. Mr. Bill Slayton has a wonderful write-up on the web with Ken Norton. You'll find it quite nice. I remember my first professional fight like it was yesterday. My sparring partner and I had worked out for weeks getting ready for our first fight as professionals. He was in another fight stable than I was but in the same gym. Man he and I would use different moves on each other anytime we would spar. We would spar at least ten rounds most times we worked out together. Some days he would win more rounds than me and sometimes I would win more rounds than him. There would be days he tired faster than I would and the same for me at times. This went on for weeks with both of us trying to out box each other. It got so everybody in the gym would makes bets on us each day on who would win. No day was the same at any time. We became evenly matched that betting on us became real competitive because we were so evenly conditioned. We were like brothers in a family that fought each other. We fought each other harder than we would fight any other fighters in the gym .We both enjoyed the competition. No other fighters in the gym could beat us in our weight class, so we trained only with each other the entire time we trained for our first fight. When fight time came we both grew excited and got in great shape. We were ready for anything.

When fight time came his trainer and my trainer and us went over to the arena at the same time even though we had different dressing rooms. We both were like lions in a cage just pacing back and forth. This was the big night of our professional debut as fighters. The only thing different was we were about 20 years apart in age and he had amateur fights and I didn't. We were so high on cloud nine. He knew what he was going to do his opponent and so did I. My plans were to knock my opponent out in the first round. What his plans were I didn't know. When we were at the gym training we only said to each other that we had plans for the first round but never discussed those plans. But we knew we had something big planned for the first round. Now to our surprise neither one our opponents showed up for the match that night. So that meant we had to fight each other. Now that I look back on that night I believe it was planned for us to fight each other but we were not in the loop to know. If we had been we might not have taken the fight because we were sparring partners and good friends. Little did I know but that happens quite often with fighters in the same gym. We weren't told we were going to have to fight each other until the last minute before we were to enter the ring. So I now know, I really thought it was planned all the time for us to fight each other. By then it was entirely too late to say no. We went into the arena, all the fans cheering wildly for both of us. We felt like gladiators in the Roman Coliseum. I had a special full-length boxing robe that said Black Kojack as well as my boxing trunks. I had special black shoes. My robe and my trunks were made of white satin with black trim. I was dressed very sharp if I my say so myself. I still have them today hanging in the closet. My family was there along with my wife and son and all my friends at ringside. My best friend Jerry Haywood since junior high was also there. My sparring partner's family and friends were there too. The ringmaster introduced us and then he sent us to our corners. I was dancing all around the ring as we were being introduced. The crowd was going wild and so were my insides. The bell rang and we both headed out to the center of the ring. I jumped around just to set up myself with my opponent right in front of me and threw my first punch. It was a right hand right to the chin. To my surprise it sent him to the canvas. The crowd went wild and I was sent to my corner as I watched my buddy roll over and get up off the floor. Man the look on his face was frightening. For the next two rounds he chased me all around that ring like an enraged madman. It was all I could do to keep him off me. I got so tired running from that guy at times I would stand in the middle of the ring and just exchange punches for a minute and then start running again. That was the hardest fight I had in my career fighting my friend. Man I sure was glad that fight was coming to an end. I hadn't been so tired in all my life even when I played football with the LA Rams. I tell you he wore me out. The crowd was just going wild the whole fight. I tried to knock him down several times but to my surprise he wouldn't go down. Frasier just kept on coming after me. Man I was so happy when that fight ended. It was like being saved from death. But you know brothers fight among themselves harder than they would fight anybody else. That fight reminded me of Muhammad Ali, and Smokin Joe Frazier who never stops coming. That was by far the hardest fight in my boxing career of 29 years. Our fight was the best fight on that boxing card that night. It was more exciting than the main event. We had everybody standing the whole fight. They were yelling and stomping with so much energy I thought there was an earthquake. That was a night I shall never forget. We both were glad when that fight was over. We hugged and kissed each other with so much relief. My other fights in my career were good also but none as memorable as the first.

After that fight I couldn't move for a few days. My best friend talked about me for weeks on end about how much I ran in that fight. He laughed and laughed at me while telling other friends of ours. Well I never did say what the outcome was in that fight; it was a draw. We both were satisfied with that decision. So again I kept in great shape even after my pro football career ended. To box professionally you had to be in tip-top shape to box three minutes for ten rounds. Even then I prided myself in being in the best condition I could be. You have to remember I was thirty years old too. In the boxing world that's real old. Most fighters are wrapping up in their boxing careers when I was just starting. It was a pleasure training with Mr.

Slayton and being recognized as a stable mate of Ken Norton. It was a lot of fun and of course I met a lot of big time boxing figures. And I was kind of a celebrity around Los Angeles at that time too. Whenever I fought in Los Angeles I would park my new 1977 Lincoln Mark V in front of the auditorium so people would know I was there. The license plate read "Kojack" which was my nickname. Those were some fun but also great times. I was married with a two-year-old son who loved to ride with his head sticking out of the sunroof.

Chapter 3: The Move

In 1982 I moved to Birmingham, Alabama. I had seen so much of the South on television through the years of racial tension in the 60s and always wanted to know what it was like to live there. From the early and late 60s there had been marches and demonstrations in Birmingham with the police using the night sticks, dogs and fire hoses. The Freedom Riders down through Alabama, Mississippi, Carolinas and Georgia and of course all the racial killings and bombings in various southern states had ended. Living in Birmingham was very pleasant. Everyone I came in contact with while I lived there whether Black or White were very kind and respectful. I enjoyed my stay in Birmingham, getting to know all the people on the Birmingham City Council as well as the City Council President Betty (Fine) Collins. She granted my license for my business Kojak's Escort Service—the first and only escort service ever run in the state of Alabama at that time.

While in Birmingham I continued to workout at the boxing gym and the weight room but never promoted fights there. I just kept my health together just in case I decided to box again. I lived in the Big Ham for two years where I got my real estate license, sold real estate and worked at a retail furniture store. I didn't care for the kind of money I was making so decided to relocate to Atlanta, Georgia. At that time in 1982 there was no job market in Birmingham. If you didn't have your own business you just couldn't find work. Even when I was at home in Los Angeles I had heard so much about Atlanta, Georgia. Good old Hot Lanta. I had heard it was wide open for young businessmen like me. I wanted in on that kind of life for myself. But the fact was the South was not all it was cracked up to be. Not Birmingham anyway. While in the Big Ham I wanted to help others who had health misfortunes so I took an EMT course at UAB for six months. I thought I was going to make it through the course. I was making pretty good grades throughout the course. I got down to the final. I studied really hard for that test and missed passing by three points. I had asked the professor to let me make the three points up somehow. But he would not budge. He said I would have to take the class all over again. I couldn't dream of going through that class from start to finish again. So I just walked away. I said Birmingham must not be the place for me. My marriage did not work and my relationship with my new daughter's mother was hitting rock bottom also so maybe Birmingham was not for me. Nothing was working for me but my health. So I thought I better get out while I was able.

In September 1985 I moved to Atlanta, Georgia not knowing a soul. Just up and left Birmingham one weekend. I knew a person in Birmingham who had a friend in Atlanta who was looking for a roommate. I got the guy's phone number and called him. He gave me directions in Atlanta to find him and I came running. I stayed with him for a while until I got on my feet on the ground and found my own place in Southwest Atlanta called Adamsville. I joined the real estate brokerage there whose owner had a place for rent in the area. I rented my broker's one bedroom over a garage. Little did I know it was not insulated at all. My broker gave me a space heater to use but the heat all went up any place below the heater kept cold. So my feet were always cold when I would walk around on the floor because heat would rise above the heater. When winter came that place froze over like an ice cycle. It was so cold I couldn't stay there. My broker had to move me to one of her other places. It got so cold everything in the place just froze. There were 12 steps from the ground to the top to the front door. Every step was covered with ice up to the front door. The door was covered with a sheet of ice so you couldn't open the screen door to get to the main door to the apartment. There was no way I could stay there. So after the freeze was over I moved to a place in Smyrna Georgia. I guess my broker thought for $25 a week what would I expect. I knew I had to keep my body in tune but I had to be stable in order to make it right.

After moving to Smyrna I started training at the Police Athletic League (PAL). PAL was located in downtown Atlanta and run by a police officer named Josh Dunlap. He was a by-the-book individual with the mentality of an Atlanta police officer. He was really good at what he did. He wanted his organization to be the best it could be. Not only was he a good old athlete but a good businessman. He helped me become the fighter I wanted to be at my age as well as gain a foothold in business so I could earn a living. While at PAL I had the pleasure of meeting a young up and coming Olympic boxer Evander Holyfield. I watched him rise from an amateur fighter into an Olympian and then to a World Champion so easily and change. The PAL organization did for him what it had done for many young Black men in Atlanta. Being a part of this organization helped me keep my health together to pursue my heights in boxing. After getting involved with PAL I grew interested in fighting pro again. I trained at the professional boxing gym in downtown Atlanta Here I met Laila Ali, Vernon Forest and other fighters with champion status. When I met Ms Ali she was getting ready to spar with another fighter. She had not put her wraps on her hands yet before sparring. She shook my hand and I noticed her hands were badly bruised and cut just like those of most pro fighters. But she was such an attractive humble and gracious woman, I couldn't believe that's what she did for a living. It takes all kinds of people to make this old world. I was expecting a pair of nice soft hands but her hands were rougher than mine. I guess you can imagine what a shock it was for me to see that. I guess that is the nature of the fight game. This gym on Spring Street in downtown Atlanta was the most popular gym for pros at that time. It was my haven to keep my body in shape. Whenever I was examined by fight doctors at that time I always received a clean bill of health.

Being a professional athlete in Atlanta Georgia had its perks, like meeting other great athletes, getting into entertainment venues free, and gaining items from large department stores at little to no cost. You could travel to sporting events outside the city with other sporting teams just because you were well-known. Being in shape certainly had its advantages. That's why I always tried my best to be in shape. Keeping away from women while you were training was hard to do. They were all over the city when you were in training it seemed. They were in the gym while you were doing your thing in the ring or on the training floor. You wanted to look good and be at your best because you knew they were watching your every move. That too made you stay in shape and healthy in your sport. I have to say it was fun trying to excel while training for a contest. Drinking wasn't too hard not to do because I didn't like alcohol anyway. I always kept my health in mind all the time on and off the court. Smoking is the one vice I never got hooked on. I remember when I was ten years old we lived in South Central Los Angeles on 23rd street and Central Ave right in the middle of the hood. It was summer time 1959. My father would send me to the liquor store to buy his cigarettes with a note saying he was sending me and what kind of cigarettes he wanted along with his signature on the note. He smoked Phillip Mores and Chesterfield Kings cigarettes all the time. After going to the store I would save his notes for myself so if I wanted some cigarettes I could get them at any time. Some of the kids I

37

hung with at the park smoked. Wanting to be a part of the group I joined in and smoked too thinking it was the thing to do. But I got caught smoking in our bathroom at home one night by my dad. Like most kids do, as you are smoking you try to fan the smoke out the window after you puff on the cigarette. It didn't work for me fast enough. I got caught right in the middle of fanning. He put the fear of God in me by telling me what he was going to do to me if he caught me smoking again. My dad didn't play when it came to punishing us boys. It was serious business. When he was through saying what he was going to do to me I never wanted to see another cigarette again. At ten years old that was pretty frightening. Though I still wanted to be a good athlete and athletes just didn't smoke if they wanted to remain healthy. From that time on I never smoked again. So I have been so health conscious since I was ten years old because I wanted so much to be that great athlete. But at the same time I certainly was afraid of what my father was going to do me. He was a pretty muscular guy during those days.

In the year 2000, I was still in excellent health and boxing at one of the Atlanta gyms. I was training three times a week just to keep in shape with no fights in the future just in case something came up. I was fifty-two years old then and boxing with the younger guys. No one knew how old I was because I didn't show in looks. I would go to the gym in Smyrna, the one in Norcross and the one in downtown Atlanta to train. I looked like all the other young guys and no one questioned my age because I looked young and was boxing with all the pros and younger guys. At that time I was not interested in a real fight. I just wanted to keep in some kind of shape. In the back of my mind I might want to fight again. I started boxing over the years with some of the best Atlanta had in my weight class. I got known all over Atlanta and fighters wanted to try me out to see how good I really was. So I would make appearances throughout the Atlanta area at the big gyms to spar other fighters that were the best in my class. This went on for a few years and finally I hit pay dirt. I got a contract to fight in Savanna, Georgia. To be able to fight again I had to go through the Georgia Boxing Commission and the Commissioner himself Tom Mishou in order to get my boxing license in 2002. He had to personally see me box before he would issue me a boxing license in Georgia because I was over fifty years old. So the Commissioner attended a sparring session I had at the Smyrna, Georgia gym. My sparring partner was Roosevelt Walker, a well-seasoned welterweight for fifteen years that the Commissioner knew. The match went for seven rounds. The Commissioner and one of his personal friends, a pro referee, watched as we worked out. Needless to say he was very impressed with my skills at fifty-two years old. I surprised myself as well as I moved and grooved. I got it all on film along with the Commissioner and I looked good if I said so myself. I was looking pretty smooth and fast. After the match the Commissioner and I greeted each other and he introduced to his friend the referee and then he gave me the green light to fight at age fifty-two.

Following my interaction with Mr. Mishou regarding my boxing license he and I became good friends in the sport of boxing. I could call on him by phone or go down to his office just to say hey. He was just easy to reach personally as a friend and always had something nice to say. After I had been given the ok to box again I called home to California to my family and told everyone the good news. There were mixed emotions among my family. But they all knew what kind of competitor I was and besides everyone knew this might be the last time I would be able to compete at a professional level. So they all gave me the go ahead. You know you have to be in great shape to box on a professional level especially at this age. One of the conditions was I would have to see a cardiologist and get a good bill of health. Well the doctor gave me a stress test along with a thorough physical examination from head to toe. The outcome of the physical was excellent. I sure was glad that it was. I was on pins and needles. So at fifty-two I was still in great shape and able to compete professionally as a boxer. I took the information back to the Commissioner and man was he surprised. He congratulated me and issued me the boxing license for one year in Georgia. A week later a fight was offered me in Savanna, Georgia. I was on top of my game and ready to fight. My manager and I went to Savanna for the fight of my last Harrah so I thought. I felt good; I wasn't tired or dragging. I felt great. We weighed in the day before the fight. It was very interesting being included in the weigh-in with all the fighters, trainers, corner men, referees and the Commissioner along with the press in one room trying to get all the fighters weighed in and matched. It was something to see, like a big party. It was really something to experience if you haven't. The fighters are sizing one another up getting on and off the scales weighing themselves. You look at them and they look at you flexing your muscles and making facial expressions all trying to

41

impress their opponent and the audience. It's quite a show. It was so funny and a lot of fun to be a part of at the time. It was part of the game and show.

The night of the fight you get butterflies thinking about what you are going to do in the fight in front of all those people. You are hoping you don't run out of gas in the first round or in any round. Unfortunately I didn't win my fight but if it was any consolation my opponent knew I was there. I couldn't get my opponent to give me a rematch no matter what I said. He wouldn't give me one. So I just let it go. I think about it oh so often. I knew it was my age that was holding the rematch back, so I just let it go. I still kept in shape. I continued to travel from gym to gym working out being the athlete I wanted to fight one more time. I knew I had it in me. So I trained even harder. In 2005 God blessed me with another fight opportunity. I was not going to blow this blessing at my age of fifty-six. Most people that didn't know my athletic ability would say I was way out of my mind to even think about it. But those who did know me knew what type of athlete I was. They knew I was on a tough track professionally. I don't remember how I obtained the contract but I had another chance to fight in April of 2005 and that was all that mattered. I was so grateful and excited I called all my family on the East Coast and West telling them the news. As it so happened my son and his family were stationed in Tennessee. He and his wife both were in the Army. They were both excited about the fight too, although my son wondered what I was doing fighting at fifty-six years old. He thought I was a little out of my mind. They wanted to come too because they had never been to a live professional boxing match and of course it was my grandchildren's grandfather's fight. Now that was different.

I traveled to the fight with my team from Atlanta, Georgia. There were other guys from my gym fighting on the same card as I was that night. The fight was held at a Latin venue in Smyrna, Tennessee. I didn't know there was a Smyrna in Tennessee until the fight. At the venue they played all Latin music and nothing else. So you know the music was very loud all night long. The crowd was 99% Latin and maybe 1% white. We were the only Blacks in the venue. The atmosphere was moving with people, music and smoke. It seemed like everyone was having a good time. The fans were very gracious to our team. It was like they knew we were not going to win any of our fights. All the gladiators were pumped up high with adrenaline flowing wild. The mood was good and I felt great and loose ready to battle. My match came up quickly and I was ready. Just before my match I found out that my opponent was a no show and they matched me up with another fighter. Little did I know my opponent was a middleweight and not a lightweight. I signed the contract as a lightweight fighter not a middleweight. I told them I didn't want to fight him because of the weight difference. They said if I didn't fight I wouldn't get paid. I had come so far; I think it was about four hundred miles. So I said to myself I can't come this far to not get paid so I took the fight. So I got myself mentally ready for the big challenge. When I stepped into the ring I became someone I didn't know. I was possessed and cocky. I completely lost it. I was someone else. I was moving so smooth and fast I couldn't keep up with myself. I thought I couldn't be stopped. I took chances I wouldn't ordinarily or normally take. I pushed myself to the very end. My opponent couldn't hit me no matter what he did. He kept missing me with every punch he threw. I made him very angry because he couldn't keep up with me nor could he hit me. I would spin him off the ropes and make him look silly every time. I knew I was a better fighter than he was and he knew it too. Then it happened—every fighter's nightmare. I got caught with a punch I didn't see. My campaign of moving in and out all around my opponent had ended. You see, he couldn't hit me no matter what he did. That gave him fits. He got pretty angry because he couldn't hit me. The grave mistake was made. I stepped in and tried to beat him toe to toe. I had forgotten he was much taller and weighed 20 lbs. more than I did. Also he was stronger than I was too. But at the time it didn't faze me at all. I wasn't thinking clearly. I just was in a zone. The dead zone. I just knew I was a better fighter than he was, or so I thought. I was but I just got careless and cocky and he caught me right on my chin. He threw a right cross right on the button (they call it in boxing right on the mark). I stood toe to toe with him and tried to take him out and lost. It was all over. I felt so foolish that I didn't take my time and beat him. I got the big head and moved too fast. It was too late for second guesses. That was my Last Harrah. Disappointing but that was life in the fast lane.

Chapter 4: Back in the Day

Since that last fight I just worked out at the boxing gym sparring with the guys and at the spa working out with the weights. On the weekends I would run on the jogging trails to keep my legs and cardio up to par. I used to run 3ks, 5ks and 10ks just to stay in shape. I've run the Atlanta Peachtree nine years in a roll. I still have all my t-shirts hanging in the closet from each of the Peachtree Road Races. This was a span from 1985 to 1994. I've run other major races 3k, 5k and 10k here in the Atlanta area too over the years. I was pretty good too if I have say so myself. One of the most fun races was the Rock and Fun Run Road Race where all the participants wore clothing of some well-known profession like doctors, nurses, firemen, and sports uniforms such as football, tennis, basketball and other professions too. I never needed or took any type of vitamins of any kind to supplement my body needs. I never took any kind of medicine at all for my health. Great health was always a blessing to me. I just kept in great shape by participating in regular physical exercise on a weekly basis along with a great diet. It was just part of my life style. All the people who knew me through work or social ties wondered how I kept in such excellent shape and health all the time. Good health seemed to follow me all my life through all seasons of work, play and business. It seems like it was a blessing from God. Sports and exercise have always been part of my way of life. I never needed enhancements of any kind to perform well ever. I just did whatever I wanted to do with my body in sports and made it happen, if you will. I believed if you trained hard and continued eating the right foods and got the proper rest your body needed, you could do what you asked of your body at your command. That has always been my creed and cradle of athleticism.

Now I remember when I was kid about fourteen years old in 1962. I was attending an all-boys high school in Watts, California, Verbum Die High School. I was one of the first 62 boys that started that Catholic boys' high school under the direction of a priest named Father Frances. Even then good health and sound bodies was a major factor for the students and faculty. We were much into sports from the beginning: football, basketball and track even though the first year we didn't compete with other Catholic boys high schools. We were all taught and stressed how important our bodies were to us as young men. At the time I was attending Verbum Dei my parents bought a home in an all-White community of Los Angeles near Imperial and Western in 1965. While at Verbum Dei I would hear about the White kids surfing. When I went to the beach with my family I would also see the young white kids my age surfing. I did so much want to learn how to surf. It just looked like so much fun. But I didn't know any white kids until we moved to our new neighborhood. That's when my parents transferred me to Serra High School in Gardena, California. Serra was predominantly an all-white Catholic boys' high school. Only a handful of Blacks attended the school in 1965. Well my dream was about to come true in learning how to surf. All the guys in my new school surfed. It was like having a new bike as a kid. Every kid has a bike. Everybody in the school had a surfboard. I remember in the ninth grade while still at Verbum Die I would hear how much strength and coordination it took to learn to ride a surfboard from the kids in my new neighborhood. It was a two-fold move in my opinion. I got better education it seemed and I learned how to surf. It was a break from being hassled most days by older kids from Watts trying to take our money while at the bus stop. We had to fight quite a few days trying to keep our money from being taken because we were Catholic school kids. We grew to be tough kids when it was all said and done. We didn't take anything from any kids while on the bus line. Believe it or not because we were taught to keep ourselves in good health and shape it helped us to beat off those kids on the bus stop from taking our bus money. They were slow compared to us which helped us fight well and run fast. So I learned how to surf and bought my first surfboard. I got to be a pretty good Black surfer. I would go to the beach with my school chums quite often during the weekends and surf. Being in good shape and health was certainly key to learning to surf. While at Serra would you believe I played football on the freshman team? I was too small to make a difference to the team but I was there. I might have been 110 lbs. soaking wet. I had a good time going to the games too. Most of the guys were pretty nice to me being such a little guy. I ran track too. I really wasn't any good but I was out there. I had fun though. For a little guy I got a lot of respect. I carried my own.

Well I need to talk about my motorcycle days before I get back to my story because it took a person with good health and body strength to handle a chopper motorcycle whether you were man or women. You see the choppers we put together back in the day weighted about

49

four to six hundred pounds. Of course it depended on how the bike was built. When I graduated from high school I wanted a chopper motorcycle rather than a car. My interest was belonging to a motorcycle club. I thought that was so hip and cool back in the day. But to handle these big monstrosities you had to be in good shape. The motorcycle club I was interested in was run by the L.A. Choppers. The president was Alton Grant a very good veteran motorcycle rider of many years. Shortly after I had shown interest in becoming as a member of the Los Angeles Choppers there was a tragic accident where Alton was killed. Alton was getting on the Harbor Freeway in Los Angeles and a motorist was backing down the same on ramp to the freeway and ran over Alton's bike killing him instantly. Now if this wasn't ironic my power lifting mentor in college whos name was Winfred Robinson was also killed on a motorcycle shortly after learning how to ride. He had no experience on bikes at all and was riding on the freeway during a raining day. He only had been riding motorcycles for three months. He should have never been on that bike during any rainy weather. Being quite older than I was you would think he had knowledge of not riding a motorcycle in the rain. Riding bikes in the rain is a BIG NO NO. Even the police don't ride their motorcycles when it rains. But I guess because he was a big strong guy he felt he had the power. Shortly after Alton's accident a new president was elected in the Choppers Motorcycle Club. He was a well-built older guy a senior member of the Choppers Bobby Johnson. Now Bobby after talking to him and letting him know my interest he said I would have to be in good shape to handle the kind of chop I wanted to build. It was going to weigh about 600lbs because of what I wanted. After I had demonstrated and told him about my physical abilities as an athlete along with my social skills as a person, he and the other members of the club decided to vote me in the club. Being part of a motorcycle club every club member has a unique motorcycle name. These are some of the names of our club members. My name being the youngest member at that time was Baby Chop. There was Pudden, there was Fast Mike, there was Big Black, there was Talk, there was Red, There was Big Slim, there was little Ray, and there was Slick Charles. There were others but I can't remember all the others' names. We had a real sharp club in Los Angeles at that time. All the women involved in motorcycle clubs in L.A. at that time thought we were the classiest motorcycle club in the city. We had the largest club building in the city. We had a lot of nice parties and did a lot of things for the community. We were on top of things

51

in Los Angeles City. That was something I wanted to be a part of ever since I was a kid seeing other clubs riding together two by two on the surface streets and freeways. There was one summer my parents took us all on trip up to Northern California to visit some relatives in San Francisco. As we were traveling on Pacific Coast Highway, one of the most famous highways in California, a group of Hells Angels rode past us going south two by two packing their women on their bikes and some were riding alone too. There must have been at least fifty bikes or more all different colors with lots of chrome. That was the most spell bounding sight I had ever seen. They were looking good. I mean they were all looking sharp. Man it was like being in the movies watching a Hells Angels Club ride by. Man it was always so exciting to watch those other Black Bike Clubs go by too—men and women riding their own Chops down the highways and city streets of Los Angeles two by two. They were all looking awesome, every one of them. That's what I wanted to do.

My dream came true with the L.A. Choppers. We were the best uniformed club in L.A. at the time. We even made a movie called the "Black Angels". You can get it on Amazon today or watch it on YouTube. Of course it was a

B movie at that time. Those were the times of good old fashioned fun. Our club would go on many rides during the winter and summer months. One summer I invited the whole club out to my grandparents' farm for a weekend in Shafter, California. We all had a ball. My grandparents and my cousins were so excited to see all the bikes on our ranch. The neighboring farms were surprised at the visit also. They all greeted the club well with open arms. It was a fun filled weekend with a lot of motorcycles. I tell you my motorcycle days were a blast. I was a student at Long Beach State College Monday through Friday and on Saturday and Sunday I was a motorcycle rider. I had the best of both worlds which required me to be in good health and in top physical shape.

Chapter 5: The Melt Down

Getting back on track… now that I had retired from professional sports I had ventured into intramural sports and trained at local boxing gyms as well as weight training gyms. Still after all these years in athletics I'm free of any type of drugs or enhancements of any kind. No vitamins to assist me to replenish my body's nourishments. My body functions on its own power. That's what it is supposed to do without any additives of any kind. Now that I was in my fifties with regular training of running, boxing and weightlifting, I was feeling and looking great—no symptoms of irregular health issues from my physicians. It was 2007 and I had applied for an electrician position with the City of Atlanta working on traffic signals in early spring. I was called by the City of Atlanta to come to work in December 2007. They gave me a complete physical then at the age of fifty-nine. I was in such great shape I didn't look or feel my age. I was doing everything like climbing ladders, pulling electrical wires, digging holes, wiring traffic signals and driving trucks. As a matter of fact I got my CDLs the same year. I was doing everything the job required. I was working in 100-degree weather during the summer and sometimes 15 degrees in mornings during the winter. My health held up through the hot summers and the cold winters without any problems through 2010.

Then in May 2010 I managed to land a job in inventory control and purchasing with the City of Atlanta Department of Public Works. This position was a desk job which I'd been trying to secure for some time. All the physical aspects of my electrical job had been eliminated. No lifting, no climbing, no pulling and wiring in the hot sun or cold weather. All that was over. Everything that I was supposed to do was done on a computer out of the weather where it was nice and cozy. But even then I continued to workout, box, run and weight train. Even then my workout schedule was part of my lifestyle and was kept up rigorously. My new job was at the North Ave maintenance station. This maintenance station was one of several that did street repair work throughout the City of Atlanta. What I did was made sure the crews at my station had all the equipment and supplies needed to perform any street repair job. With this job there was no strain on the body at all. A computer and a telephone were the tools needed for the job. The position was a very sweet one if I say so myself, unlike my electrician job at Clair Drive yard where the job was not difficult at all but the people were. Some of them were so hard to work with for many reasons. First of all most of the men were hardcore from broken homes and underprivileged areas. Many had criminal backgrounds of one sort or another. To work with this caliber of men was new to me with challenges which I had to adjust to quickly or get run over. Now I was no saint either; I had my faults too. I was a pussy cat compared to most of the guys I worked with. One thing I never did was bring my personal problems or concerns to work at any time. That was a no no. I was too private to do that. It got so I dreaded going to work each day because I was going to face some uneasy personal challenges with one of the guys. I believe that was one of the reasons I became sick and almost had a heart attack because it was a mental strain and pressure on me each day to go to that job and perform. You see, some of the guys I thought brought their personal problems to work with them, and before you got to the work at hand that was assigned you had to deal with your partner's issues and concerns. I was so tied up inside I just didn't ever want to go to the job because I knew what I was going to deal with when I got there day after day. My health was decreasing slowly but surely each day during the first year and a half at Clair Drive for the City of Atlanta. It would bother me so much having to go to work each day I would have cold sweats each night. I would have to change clothing about two to three times every night. It got so bad it was just draining me of everything I had. My clothes would be so wet each time I went into the sweats I could wring them out into buckets of water. I was having headaches along with night sweats too. For a while I couldn't figure out why this was happening to me. One day it hit me like a ton of bricks. I said I know why I was having so many sleepless nights with those headaches. It was the job that was getting next to me. So I talked to my supervisor and requested another position within our organization for which I was qualified. I was told by the supervisor that I would surely not like the change of yard I would be sent because it would be rougher there than it was at Clair Drive. So I decided to stay there at Clair Drive. A position was granted to me and I started working at it almost immediately. It was an inventory control and purchasing position which I had done before I came aboard with the City of Atlanta. Man! That was a relief from the pressures I was under for so long. I was able to work alone and with none of the people with whom I was having all those problems. It was so nice to be away from all the riff raff of the men who brought all their issues and personal concerns to the work place.

It was nice for a while but I wasn't far enough from the real problem. Some of the guys grew jealous and started moving in on me because I was working on the inside and not in the streets anymore. Another male employee and I got into a physical altercation, which caused me some problems. It got to be a knock out drag out physical fight. Fortunately I was able to hold my own under the pressure and not get hurt. I didn't want to get hurt so I just held the guy so he wouldn't hurt me until someone pulled us apart. I was suspended along with the other guy for three days even though I was defending myself and didn't initiate the confrontation. It didn't matter if you didn't start a fight but were involved you got disciplined also. That's the way it was with the City of Atlanta. I even took the matter to civil court, but lost and it was thrown out because I didn't have a witness to who started the physical altercation. So I just took it with a smile and moved on. Good guys don't always take first place or win. All part of life's trials and tribulations. Now because all that happened with me at Clair Drive I don't want my readers to think I thought I was better than any of my co-workers there. Not at all because I came from the same neighborhoods they did but in another state, California. You see I grew up with the same element. I was brought up in South Central Los Angeles. You can't get more hood than that. I just handled my personal issues myself and not with my co-workers. My parents taught me well how to handle myself as an adult and to accept responsibility for my actions and not take things that are not mine from others.

I was transferred to another maintenance yard on North Ave. I was told it was the roughest maintenance yard in the city and I was not going to like at all. As it turned out it was a breath of fresh air, just what I was looking for a place to work in peace and harmony. The men and women that worked at North Ave were so pleasant to work with I thought I was on another planet. It wasn't anything like I was told. I didn't know at the time but I was sent to North Ave with the idea I wouldn't make it at all. With the men and women being so tough, I was not expected to handle it. The powers that be at Clair Drive wanted me to fall flat on my face. It turned out to be just the right place for me to work. I worked close with three women. My manager Mrs. Bishop tried to carry herself as a real strict manager. She wanted to show others she was a no-nonsense manager but in reality she was a real pussycat. I was able to see straight through her and capture her heart. I knew the truth about her. She knew I knew the real deal. I never let on to the truth to others to keep her pride about her work ethic. She was pleasant every day and things always went well. Sometimes I felt guilty for getting paid for what I did every day. She was mine from then on. She gave me assignments with due dates and that was it. She never micromanaged me ever. She knew from the start she could count on me to deliver assignments when asked. From the beginning it was my game til the very end. We had a very tight employee relationship. She would always invite me out to lunch.

My favorite girls Bernadette and Richdean would always be kidding me about my relationship with Mrs. Bishop and would also talk about Mrs. Bishop and how uncompromising she was. I just ate it up and smiled inside. A year later after I left North Ave Mrs. Bishop passed on without anyone informing me that she had. I'm always going to miss her dearly. She always had such a sweet smile on her face. My health just started improving as soon as I started working at North Ave Yard. My manager and my co-workers were all so nice and friendly. I had no more night sweats and headaches. It was night and day between Clair Drive and North Ave. Yard. I worked projects in inventory control and purchasing—something I knew and enjoyed working with. Even though I worked with two women closely, I basically worked alone. That's the way I truly wanted it and I truly had it like that. I really made all my own decisions about what I did in inventory control and purchasing because I knew what Mrs. Bishop wanted every month. So things went real smoothly for me all the time every day. I went to lunch when I wanted to and left the yard when I pleased. I mean I had it going on every day. People were amazed at how well I had it since I hadn't been there very long at all. I had a very good rapport with the yard maintenance chief. Everyone who had some clout I knew at North Ave word got back to Clair Drive Yard I was doing so well at North Ave that co-workers and supervisors were getting pretty jealous of my status. Their plan had backfired as I was doing just great at my new work place.

I felt great relief physically when I got over to North Ave but by then it was too late. The damage was already done to my brain cells. My left side of my brain was ready to burn. It was a time bomb waiting to explode. Those two and half years of mental abuse at Clair Drive had already done their damage, along with the way I treated my body with the daily food intake. You see I was taking in too many dairy products that were clogging up my arteries and veins with plaque and I had a high cholesterol rate to top it

61

off. That was killing me along with stress. My brain cells on the left side of my brain weren't getting proper amounts of blood and oxygen because of the plaque blockage which was leading toward a stroke. Even though things were going smoothly and easily and everything was rosy and sweet. The process was still in motion and nothing could stop it. The time was approaching for my falling. I was really getting into my job. I enjoyed the environment in which I was working. The people I worked with on a day-to-day basis were pleasant and enjoyable to work with. The tasks I performed were interesting. I was taught the Hansen software program. With this program software I could take it anywhere in the United States and use it. So I had a skill I could take with me and perform for life. My manager Mrs. Bishop wanted to show me other software programs to work with to assist her with her work duties. That's the way it was for ten months at my new job location. So I felt there was no strain on myself. So after leaving the stressful environment from the past 2.5 years, I thought my brain was healthy. Wrong! All the trash in my brain that I had endured in the past two years had been collecting. It was a time bomb ticking just waiting to explode. I was really in denial that something was about to happen. My thoughts were I had gotten rid of the pressure on me, so there was nothing to worry about. Wrong! But there was nothing I could feel or see. The silent killer called stroke was lurking near like a thief in the night waiting to strike.

It was Tuesday February 15, 2011. Just like any other Tuesday work day, I woke up at 6:00 AM and went to the bathroom, washed my face, brushed my teeth and shaved. Then I sat and read my Bible for 15 or 20 minutes, put on my work clothes, and headed out the door while picking up my lunch and juice from the kitchen. I was off to work at 7:15 AM sharp, got into my Camaro and drove to work. I made my way to the main traffic flow on South Cobb Drive headed to 285, the freeway toward downtown Atlanta. I arrived at work on time to say my good mornings and start my work day on my computer. The day went real smoothly without any hitch whatsoever. The girls and I had a fun time working together, laughing a lot along with plenty of business. We ordered equipment and supplies for the yard that day. I entered a few new parts and equipment into the Hanson system for crew use. At the end of the day I left my office while saying my usual good nights to my office crew as I headed down to the yard's break room. This is where all the crews in the yard would congregate after the work day was done at 4:30 PM. Once I arrived at the break room I started talking with one of the guys Eddie Johnson. We always picked up where we left off in the conversation from the day before. This day it was about a late 1960s folk singer who talked a song rather than sang a song. We both were supposed to do research the night before and find out who this folk singer was. When the subject came up neither one of us could remember who this person was even though we both did our research. The subject matter of this folk singer had been ongoing for a couple of weeks. As it happened we both did our homework but got nowhere. We knew he played a guitar and a harmonica which hung around his neck in the mid to late sixties. I knew in my mind who he was, but I just couldn't say his name. I could see him a clear as day. So I called my source at home, my brother Bruce. I knew he would know, because he kept up with stuff like that in music in the sixties. My brother got it right on his first guess when I asked him. He said it was Bob Dylan. I told my brother I just couldn't say his name, but I could see his face plain as day. I mentioned to Bruce I had racked my brain trying to say his name. We both came up with the folk singer Bob Dylan when we came together that day. We both congratulated each other and started talking, slapping each other's hands because we were excited about our findings after two weeks of research. Well it came time to leave for home so we shook hands, laughed, said our goodbyes and left the break room. I felt the fulfillment of the day and headed for my Camaro about 4:35pm to go home.

On my way home I thought about going to the weight room over at Life College to work out in the gym and what I was going to do while there. The drive was nice and sunny going home with very light traffic on the freeway. I had such pleasant thoughts of work that day and of the people with whom I worked. Thoughts of life in general were nice, unlike the thoughts I had when I was working at Clair Drive. My mind was at ease and free of anything that might upset me in any way. I was feeling great. I mean I was feeling so good about life, I had no worries I thought. But was I wrong. Something had been pressing me, something I was not aware of. I was driving home in a pleasurable mood. I pulled into my driveway and parked my car in front of my garage door. I felt fine sitting inside my car kind of thinking about my drive home. I got out of the car and suddenly I felt dizzy and light headed. My eyes grew blurry. My head started spinning. My right arm became uncomfortable. It started moving on its own and I couldn't stop it from flapping up and down. My right

65

leg became numb and uncontrollable. When I tried to take a step my leg would kick out to the right and collapse under me. I started getting scared. I said to myself "What's going on? "What's happening to me?" As I tried to walk away from the car my right leg kept kicking out to the right as I tried to walk. It would not go straight in a normal fashion. My right arm had a mind of its own. I couldn't control it at all. I couldn't hold on to anything in my right hand. I couldn't close the car door with my right hand. As big as the car door was I could not grab it to shut it. Each time I tried to grab the car door and shut it I would reach for it and miss it with my right hand. As a matter of fact I had to use my left hand to hold on to things to stand and walk. Once I opened up the garage door with the garage opener I entered, holding on to the walls to get to the back door steps with rails leading to my house back door. Once I climbed the stairs using my left hand and left leg I pulled myself to the top of the stairs. Once I got to the top I tried to grab hold of the door knob with my right hand. But I kept missing it. I just couldn't grab hold of the door knob. No matter how hard I tried I kept missing the door knob with my right hand. It just wouldn't cooperate. It just kept moving on its own. I had a hard time using my key to open the door. I kept dropping the keys once I got them out of my pocket. I couldn't hold on to them. I tried to pick them up off the floor with my right hand and I couldn't grab them no matter how hard I tried. It was scary to say the least. So I had to use my left hand to pick the keys up and to open the door. Now as it was I had lost control of my right arm and my right leg. They just moved on their own and I had no way of controlling them. So finally they stopped moving and I got control of my limbs again my arms and my legs. I thought to myself *what the hell just happened. I'm just hungry* I thought because I didn't really eat a good lunch that day. (I didn't know with my bright self I was having a stroke.)I thought about staying home because of what had happened but I decided to go on to the gym anyway because I felt alright now. I just couldn't figure out what had just happened to me. So I got myself a little something to eat and went on to the gym. On my way to the gym I felt fine with something on my stomach so I felt I would be able to work out.

After getting to the gym at Life College and parking my car and walking to the center I felt fine. Right in the middle of my workout I started feeling again like I felt before at home. Right on the workout floor I started getting dizzy and losing my motor skills in my right arm and leg. The weights became difficult to handle. I said to myself not again "What's wrong with me?" I thought it would go away but it didn't. (I didn't mention but the first time this happened my speech was slurred too when I was talking to myself as things were going on.) My arm started moving on its own and my leg started kicking out to the right when I tried to walk. I said to myself *I got to get out of here without people thinking I'm spastic or something.* I was embarrassed to let people see me like this. The gym was full of mostly young people and women. I just didn't want to be seen like this. You know something being seriously wrong with me just didn't occur to me at all. That's why I didn't call out for help. Little did I know I was having another stroke. I just kept it to myself and tried to make my way out to my car without bringing any attention to myself. So I took a deep breath and worked my way from the men's locker room to the water fountain in the middle of gym like I needed a drink. Then I worked my way to the front door and then outside. My car was about a quarter of a mile up a hill in the parking lot. It was dark and cold with the wind blowing. It was so cold, about 30 degrees and dark. This time of the year in February about 6 pm it got dark early. I got so tired trying to walk on my right leg up a hill as it kept kicking to the right while collapsing and my

68

.

right arm was uncontrollable too. While walking I fell a few times trying to hold myself up. My right leg kept giving out on me. The last time I fell I just laid there hoping someone would happen by and help me. That didn't happen. Man! It was so dark and cold. I was freezing all over. I just didn't know whether I was going to make it or not to my car, but I had to just lay there until I could pull myself together to move further to my car up the hill. I finally found my way to my car by crawling on all fours. It took some time but I finally made it. I crawled into my car and I said "What the hell is going on with me?" I was scared stiff, but I still kept myself under control. I was trying to figure out what was happening to me and why. A stroke did not even cross my mind. I always thought I was in such great shape. I always had exercised and eaten well so I knew I was fit. I was in the dark because I didn't know what a stroke was. No! I had no idea what a stroke was.

After getting into my car I realized I couldn't use my right arm and my right leg to drive. Thus, I used my left arm to handle the steering and my left leg to handle the accelerator. It was very strange but I got it together working the gas and brake with my left leg. I had to say to myself "Can I make it home driving like this in the dark?" I said "I can if I want to get home in one piece." I started my car up and let it warm up a while before I moved it. Since I was doing everything with my left side I had to do everything slowly. I wanted to make it home in one piece. When I figured the car was warmed I eased it out the parking space, backing up using my mirrors on my left and right sides. Clearly I was missing all the cars parked on my right and left sides. Once I had straightened out the car from the parking space I eased out the maze of the parking lot into the main stream of traffic flow. I made my way out of the school grounds on to the main street of the city on South Cobb Drive in Marietta and headed home slowly at about 20 miles an hour. I stayed in the slow lane just moving along as carefully as I could. All the cars were going around me because I was going too slow for everyone. That was alright with me because I just wanted to get home safe and sound in one piece. At the same time my right arm and my right leg were moving around on their own just as they were before and my eyes were not very clear. I was in the midst of another stroke and I couldn't stop them so I just let them go and concentrated on the road getting home. This was one of the scariest times of my life trying get home in this physical condition alone. I didn't know or have any type of idea what my body was going to do at any time. So

I just prayed that I would make it home while driving and looking all around me at the cars that were traveling alongside of me. Thank God I made it home without any incidents or issues while driving with half of my body not working. What was in my favor was I was able to catch all the green lights along South Cobb Drive all the way home until I turned off into my neighborhood on Church Road in Smyrna.

As soon as I got home and got in the house my arm and my leg stop moving just like that. I was so scared. I called my girlfriend Ms. C and told her what I had just been through since I had gotten off work. She was so amazed at what I had explained to her that she couldn't believe it. After I had convinced her that what happened to me did indeed happen to me, I told her I was so afraid it was going to happen again and if I could come over to her place to spend the night in case. Of course she was afraid for me and said it was alright for me to stay with her for the night. She also asked me if I called my doctor and told him what was happening to me. I told that I hadn't called yet because it was too late at night. Also I told her when this was happening I didn't think it was all that serious so didn't try to get help. I thought I was just light headed because I hadn't had a good lunch. She replied telling me not to let that happen again without calling my doctor. Something serious could have been going on inside my body and I could have died. That night I slept very well with no problems at all. The next morning all was well. It was like it never happened and I went to work. When I got to work that morning I called and tried to get an appointment with my doctor at my Kaiser location but none were available. So I got to see another doctor at another Kaiser location after work that day. I told this doctor what had transpired with me the day before, but she didn't seem to be too concerned even after I told her how my body was reacting. She just looked at me without even examining me and gave me some high blood pressure medicine and sent me home. She mentioned nothing about a stroke so how was I supposed to convince her something major had just happened to me that was life threatening? I went home with my meds and took one a day as I was told. So for the next two days everything went well with no problems or issues.

The third day Friday February 18, 2011 I woke up energetic and happy to go to work. The morning was fresh and sunny. I had fixed my lunch the night before and had it ready to pick up as I hit the back door the next morning. I had a great night's sleep and was ready to go. I was looking forward to having a great time with my fellow work buddies at work. We always had something to talk about along with a lot of laughter. The people made the work place enjoyable. It was always something new every day. That's what made it so interesting because the people you work with brought so many interesting things to see and to talk about every day. There was not ever a day that was the same. As usual I would leave my building about 4:00PM and head down to the break room after saying my goodbyes to my office work crew. Once I got to the break room I would find one of my buddies who on this day it happened to be Eddie Jones. We always had something profound to talk about most days. This was not one of those days. Our conversation was extemporaneous. It was fun and interesting. We laughed and talked about everything that came to our minds. It was Friday so we were going to let it all hang out. And we did. We had so much fun at our table that others around started joining in. There was so much fun and laughter. Then it was time to leave for home. I hated to leave the job. The day was nice, sunny and clear. The weather was so pleasant. You couldn't have asked for a nicer day. I was feeling great physically with no issues of any kind. I walked to the parking lot and got into my car and started home. I rolled down my window to get some of that fresh afternoon air along with the sunshine. It was great riding home. Not a care in the world, just feeling good about my place of work and the kind of work I was doing, having a great day with my fellow employees. Just a grand feeling about what I was doing to make a living and where my work place was and of course the people I was working with. I had such a pleasant ride home on the freeway with the traffic moving so smoothly.

I finally made it home and I turned into my driveway and pulled in front of my garage sitting in my car thinking about going to the gym and working out. I stepped out of my car and stood up and WHAM! It hit me just like it did Tuesday three days ago, right at the same spot and time. My head started spinning, my right arm started moving on its own, my right leg started kicking to the right when I would take a step, my speech started slurring, my lips puckered up. I still didn't know what was happening to me. So I made my way into the house as I did the first time this happened. All this was going on about 5:15 PM. I was getting scared. I knew something was truly wrong. I then managed to get to my back door steps and pull my way up to the door. Using my left hand to find my keys and open the door, I tried to call 911 and guess who was on the line. That's right! It was my doctor trying to call me. He must have gotten word of my visit Tuesday and was checking on me to see how I was getting along. As I was telling him what was happening to me right then, he told me to hang up the phone and call 911 immediately. I did just as he said to do and within five minutes or so the fire department was at my door along with an ambulance.

After I talked to my doctor I called Ms. C and told her what was happening to me and she came over right away. She came in right after the Fire Department had arrived. I asked her to call my brother Bruce and my son Keidri to let them know that I had grown ill but not to worry. The rescue team came in through the back door from the garage with all their equipment, examined me, strapped me down to a gurney and wheeled me out to ambulance. They wasted no time getting me to the hospital over at Cobb General. Once there they took me through a battery of tests, checking me out to see what had caused my reaction. They kept me at Cobb General under observation all night until early Saturday morning. They still didn't tell me what was wrong with me. I remember the ambulance crew waking me up about 2:00 or 3:00 AM that Saturday morning letting me know they were getting ready to transport me to another facility after all those examinations. Ms. C was in the room with me at Cobb General comforting me because I was very frightened. I didn't know what to expect from the traumatic experience of the third physical reaction. She was very good in keeping me calm and relaxed. At this time I still didn't know what was causing my body to react this way. Early that Saturday morning about 3am they started moving me to anther facility. Finally I asked the ambulance crew where they were taking me. They replied over to Northside Hospital off the 285 freeway. I can remember it was very cold that morning. The ride over to the hospital was a long ride. I had an African American EMT woman riding with me in the back of the ambulance who was talking to me trying to keep me cool and relaxed. Ms. C followed the ambulance to the hospital. By that time we were all so tired and I know Ms. C was plum tuckered out. I told her thanks for staying with me. She had to work that Saturday too. So I asked her to go on home; I would be alright. "Just call me later Saturday some time when you get a chance. "

Chapter 6: The Northside Hospital Challenge

Once I was settled in my permanent room at Northside I felt more relaxed and relieved I was in good hands. I was so exhausted and tired I fell asleep for the rest of that early morning. I woke up about 8 or 9 AM on February 19th and realized that my whole right side of my body was immobile. *What's happening to me* I thought. I couldn't move my arm, my wrist, my fingers, my leg, my toes. I couldn't speak when I tried to talk to myself to see if I was in a dream or something and my eyes were blurry too. I thought then it was a dream. I didn't know what was going on. I wondered how I got like this. I managed to get through the rest of Saturday alone because I slept. I got very frightened and frantic on Sunday after awaking and finding my right side of my body was in fact immobile and realizing it was not a dream. I went plum ballistic with the nurses trying to calm me down but couldn't. They tried to call Ms. C to let her know I was freaking out and if she could come and get me to relax. They were able to reach her and she came to see me. Man! That was such a relief to see her smiling face to know I had someone with me at this frighten state I was in. I tried to talk to her but my words were slurred and not clear. I couldn't hold anything in my right hand not even a plastic spoon or fork. I had tears in my eyes and she could see I was frightened and confused because of my state of mind. You can imagine how I felt being a strong and healthy person all my life then all of a sudden not being able to move one's limbs one day for some unknown reason. What a shock to me this was. She smiled and looked at me saying it was going to pass, trying to assure me as she did. I knew she had no idea what was wrong with me though I was just glad she was there. So finally the doctor came to see me and told me what was going on with me. With Ms. C listening he said I had a stroke on my right side of my body and that it was not reversible. Devastating as the news was my whole life just passed through my mind so clearly like everything happened yesterday—all the things I did as a child to my present time of my life. It was so strange to be able to see your pass life so vividly in an instant and with such clarity too. I saw all the things I did as a child leading up to my adulthood that was meaningful to me. I had heard of people seeing their lives pass right before their eyes in a traumatic state of mind. I never thought it was true, but it is a fact you can because I did. I felt my life was over and I cried like a baby. I thought to myself what was going to become of me not being able to move my right side of my body ever. So I just laid there numb without any feeling at all with tears running down my face. I thought to myself *nobody is going to want to be with me in this state, nobody. I am going to be a burden to my family. I'm going to wind up being alone for the rest of my life. What am I going to do?* Ms. C did her best trying to console me and make me feel better. I did pull myself together and come to terms with my condition. Ms. C couldn't stay with me long on Sunday because she had to work that day. She did have her brothers and the oldest brother's wife come visit me later that day.

After everyone left Sunday I had a chance to reflect on what just happened to me which would be life changing forever. Also I remember asking Ms. C to call my family at home in California. I told her to tell them I was alright and not to worry about me, because I was in good hands and not to spend the money to come out here to see me. I was doing fine. I really wanted them here with me but I was just putting on a tough act. They would have come if I had given the ok to come.

After the smoke cleared and I settled down, I came to grips with myself and I said to myself, "This is the way

God wants it to be so who am I to cry about it. I still have my life and it could be worse". So I did everything I needed to with my left hand. While at Northside Hospital I had my own private room with a sitter 24 hours a day for seven days. I had a new sitter every 8 hours that would help me with everything I needed for seven days. I never had the same sitter twice. I mean any and everything I needed, whether it was washing my face in the morning, brushing my teeth, shaving, eating, putting on my clothes–they were there to help. You see I couldn't get out of my bed. If I had to use the restroom I would get a bed pan to do my business in every morning. Man did I hate that every day. That was the most embarrassing thing for me. The sitter would have to give me the bed pan and then the nurse would have to clean me up when I finished. Every day this was the drill. By the third day I had the sitter put me in a wheelchair and wheel me into the rest room and sit me on the stool. I would do my business and use my left hand to clean myself up. After that they would come in, help me off the stool and into my wheelchair to go wash my hands and then wheel me back to my bed. You see! All the sitters I had every day were so comforting all the time. They all catered to my every need. Even if it was 2 or 3 o'clock in the morning they would be happy to help me with anything I needed. I was so surprised at their willingness to assist me at any time, but that's the way they were trained. That was their job to help me with all my needs. I was sure they got paid very well for what they dd. They did everything with a smile, even in the wee hours. They were great sitters. We had such a great rapport with each other they wanted to sit with me at home when I got out of the hospital.

The entire time I spent at Northside Hospital was purely observational on what type of stroke I suffered. They were also watching me and taking me through examinations of various types to see if I was in line for other strokes. Through those tests and watching me they were making a determination whether I was a good candidate for rehabilitation. No matter how hard I tried I wasn't able to use my right side of my body. I was trying speak every day but couldn't. I tried to eat and swallow which was very difficult. They would not give me any solid foods because I couldn't perform normal eating functions at all. I would choke when I tried to eat and drink. I tried to move my arm, my hand and move my fingers, my leg which did not seem to be able to move either. Those brain cells on the left side all were just dead that provided those functions. So every day at Northside Hospital was exhausting trying to get my limbs working again. I felt I was lost in the sauce with no hope for recovery.

My stay at Northside Hospital was going to be a few days away from home so I thought. Now my getting sick left me in a precarious situation. Now you know God reveals everything you do in the dark at some point in time to the light. This was one of those times. Usually this occurs when you least expect it. This was that time. I was dating two women and neither one knew they were in a three- way relationship. I got myself into this predicament in 2006 prior to my getting sick. I was seeing a women cross town for about five or six years whose name was Ms. V. I fell in love with the woman and I couldn't leave her no matter how badly she treated me. She had a hold on me that no other woman has ever had on me in my life. I just couldn't let go no matter what she said or did to me. I just loved being with that woman. I was really as they say in the hood pussy whipped. I was too embarrassed to let anyone know that I was, especially her. So I went krogering one afternoon hoping I would meet someone who could fill that void I had with Ms. V and met another woman who had some of the fine attributes I wanted in a woman. By chance this woman lived in my neighborhood. Her name was Ms.

C. So if I wanted to spend time with her I could because she only lived five minutes from me. This arrangement I had with both women was great. I would never get them crossed up, because they lived way cross town from each other. I had the best of both worlds with these women. They both had some qualities that I liked in women that I was looking for in one. That was something I never could find in one. So what better way to get all that you want in one than to have two with some of each. I was in hog heaven for five good years. Man I loved it. All my friends who knew me well were envious of me and how well I kept my ladies apart. I was doing just fine with them both. Holidays were the most difficult times to be away from one to be with the other. But I always found a way to make it happen. Valentine's Day was the most difficult, but I always found a way to make them both happy. I would spend that day with the one I wanted the most at that time. I made sure they both had cards, flowers and candy from me. Man I thought I was better than Mom's apple pie. I had it going on for a long time until God stopped me in my tracks with a stroke. My wonderful ride ended. While at Northside Hospital how was I going to keep them from meeting up visiting me? Well as it would happen I found out who was into me more. The lady who lived across town Ms. V didn't want to see me as badly as the woman who lived in my neighborhood did. The lady across town felt it was too far to see me often and the lady in my neighborhood Ms. C didn't feel that way at all. She would see me as often as she could when she wasn't working. That let me know who was in my corner when I needed them. I remember when I arrived at Northside Hospital I called Ms. V and told her I was in the hospital because of a stroke. You know she didn't believe me after I told her. I had to literally try and convince her I was telling the truth. At last I was able to make her understand I was indeed in the hospital. My feelings were hurt that Ms. V didn't believe me when I told her I was in the hospital. I said to her "Why would I make up a story like that to tell you?" I said to her. "That's not MO to do something like that," I told her. But I got no reply. I got a little upset at her not believing me. As it turned out anyway I was able to keep them both apart while in the hospital both at Northside and North Fulton. I had them come on different days and nights to visit me. So it worked out great. I don't know how it did, but it did. Now understand I 'm not proud about being able to handle both of those women the way I did. I just wanted to be comfortable with one woman but my first woman Ms. V didn't give me all the kinds of affection that I wanted or do all the things that I wanted done for me. So I ventured out in search of one that did do the things for me that I wanted done. I found that woman in my own neighborhood. You see I couldn't cook and my cross town woman Ms. V wouldn't cook for me at all. That bothered me a lot. I couldn't get her to cook no matter what I said or did. She was damn good in bed though, so I settled for that gift and she was a nice looking lady too. She was nice to be seen with when we went out on the town. So I settled for what I had at the time and made it work for me. Also what was a concerned to me were the feelings Ms. V had for me when I got to Northside Hospital and told her my situation. It shocked me that she didn't believe me No matter how I said it she didn't believe me. I had never been sick enough to go to the hospital ever during our relationship, so you would think she would think for what and when, but I still loved her greatly. I'll revisit this subject later in my story, because both of them would make my life comfortable later down the road. I couldn't have made it without them both during my healing process.

Getting back to my stay at Northside Hospital, every day I would be sent through a battery of tests to check my body for other blood clots. My sitters would be there to assist me with whatever I needed. Every day I would try to get the parts of my body that weren't functional back in motion. It was a difficult thing for me being laid up in bed not able to move my right side. I thought of how I used to be and what I was going to be in the future. It wasn't the easiest or best of times. I just dreaded the thought of becoming an invalid at this time of my life when I was so much into athletics and keeping my health together. I would cry every night and wonder if I was ever going to work myself out of this awful dream. It certainly didn't look good. I would think about all the people I had seen cripples recently and earlier in my life time. Would I wind up like them or what? Nobody was in my thoughts but me and God. I really didn't know what to say to God—whether I should ask for forgiveness or ask Him to cure me of this awful illness or both, because I didn't think I deserve to be left like this. I tried to do the right thing in my short life. I know I wasn't a saint but surely I wasn't so bad that I deserved this from God. So finally I just accepted the way things were and hoped there was a way out. If there was a way out I was going to really work on it to the max. The days went slowly while at Northside Hospital, because there was no progress with me I thought. Each day I just cried and felt sorry for myself cause I saw no way out of this bad situation I was in. Things looked hopeless. My prayers didn't get answered. So finally my stay came to an end. All the nurses on each shift came in my room to wish me well when they came in to work. You see I had developed a great closeness with all the nurses that attended to me during my stay there at Northside. They took good care of me and did a lot of special things for me over the period of my stay there. It was like being in a hotel on vacation. I got excellent care from all the staff. I had gotten word they were going to send me to North Fulton Hospital for my rehabilitation. Now all stroke patients don't earn a ticket to rehab hospital so I was told. So I must have been one of the fortunate ones. There must have been something they saw that made the doctors think that I had a chance to recover and get my limbs back. Whatever it was I'm so glad they saw it in me. No complaints from me whatsoever. I was ready to go. Show me the door to rehab.

Chapter 7: Rehab Hospital

On February 23, 2011 they transported me to North Fulton Hospital that evening. It was a brisk cold night and the ride was quiet and smooth in the ambulance, very pleasant. The attendants didn't talk much if at all, just doing their jobs. I guess late at night there is not much to say. Once we got to North Fulton hospital I got settled in my private room and they gave me something to eat. I had to be fed, because I was still unable to use my right side. They dressed me in my bed clothing along with some type of socks that were supposed to keep clots from forming in my legs. They ordered me to stay in bed. If I needed to go to the bathroom or get out of bed for any reason I had to call a nurse. I had three different nurses each day for each shift. They all would watch me like a hawk to make sure I obeyed the rules at all times. Man! They were real strict with me. They were on me from the very start. No slack at all. They all had their rules I had to follow. The number one rule was, do not get out of bed without a nurse. Their reasoning at that time was I couldn't walk at all and of course they didn't want me to injure myself. That was a high possibility if I got too busy by myself. So in the bed I stayed until I had a nurse help me do whatever I needed done. Now every day I would have a speech therapist, occupational therapist and a physical therapist help me use my limbs again along with speaking and eating solid foods. I had a lot to learn in a very short time. They were good no matter who I had. After the rehabilitation time they would send me home and forward me to a private therapy office location. That would cost me an arm and a leg if I had to visit them for a long while. So I wanted to learn what I needed to know to be independent at home. Many patients who suffer from strokes remained with physical therapy clinics for some time. That's not something I wanted to happen to me. For one reason my pockets were not that deep and it behooved me to learn as much and fast as possible before they sent me home. So I got on the stick and mastered everything I needed to know quickly. Being a professional athlete helped me greatly because I pushed myself all the time.

A normal day would look something like this. First I would get my breakfast, then the nurse would have me eat something and learn how to chew on both sides of my mouth real thoroughly without leaving any food in pockets of my mouth, then swallow my food slowly so to not choke.

Then I would get my speech therapist. That person would take me through a series of words to pronounce and to want me to form my words with my mouth and say them clearly, because I was really mush mouth with everything I said. So I had to clear that up so people could understand whatever I said. Then they had me read some lines from the book she had aloud so I could hear myself say the words as I read them. Then I would know what I was reading and saying was what I read correctly. I certainly didn't want to embarrass myself when people were listening to me read, so I had to practice a lot. I was terrible when I started; I mean terrible, but I got it together.

Next I would get the Occupational Therapist who would teach me how to hold and use eating utensils as well as a pen and pencil in my hand. It was foreign to me to hold eating utensils in my hand to eat. I just didn't know how to hold them. I kept dropping them in my plate or on the floor just like a baby would. I could not believe I was doing it. I knew not to but I just couldn't hold on to them. I cried because I thought I couldn't make myself handle it, but I finally got it right. Man I was so relieved I cried. Using a pen and pencil was even more difficult. I could not get holding the pen or the pencil in my hand. It was so difficult to do. I just couldn't do it no matter how hard I tried. Practicing every day and night was what it took to master writing again. I thought I would never write again with efficiency. Working at it every day made it happen. I understood what a child goes through again when learning how to use a pen or pencil. I was taught how to wash up and use a toothbrush, comb and brush what little hair I had. They showed me how to put my clothes on with buttons, zip up my pants and tie my shoes. Now that was something that was so difficult trying to button my shirt and tie my shoes. I didn't think that would be so hard, but it was. I had the damndest time trying to tie my shoes. It was so foreign to me. I just couldn't get those loops. My fingers were all thumbs; I had no dexterity. I could not make those loops and ties at all. After a few days of frustrating myself I finally got it. I said "So this is what it was like when I first learn to tie my shoes." I couldn't believe that it was so difficult to tie my shoes as a kid. But it was. Now trying to button my shirt was really difficult too, it was not a picnic. I couldn't get my fingers to work right, that almost had me crying, because I just couldn't get the button in the hole to complete the task of closing my shirt. It took me two days to button my shirt myself. My fingers were so tired along with my wrists on both hands. I never knew how difficult it was to be a child growing up putting on your own clothes, worrying about your shoes being tied and your strings coming loose, worrying about your zipper on your pants not being up. I bet those times were tough. I know I wasn't the neatest kid in school.

Next I was given a Physical Therapist, who taught me to use my arms, legs and hands again. That person would take me through a battery of finger exercises to improve my dexterity. Also that person would work on the movement of my arm and the flexibility of both my leg and arm. That person would also teach me how to walk again, just like teaching a child. It was something to behold. It was like being a child again and starting from scratch learning how to do the simplest things we take for granted every day. It was something to experience. I never thought it would be so difficult, but indeed it was. I had to walk around the therapy room in a walker under supervision. It was challenging trying to put one foot in front of another to move in a straight line. Then I had to walk up and down stairs without help, first on the right side and then on the left side and then walking up and down stairs without holding on the rails. Then I was given the task of walking the entire floor around the hospital several times a day. So my training was very rigorous to say the least. This was my routine every day for two and a half weeks to prepare myself to go home to the real world by myself.

The most important day of my stay at North Fulton Hospital was the very first morning I woke up after my evening arrival. My doctor Dr. Harbin came to my bedside that morning, introduced himself and told me all I needed to know about my condition and what he could do. He said I had suffered a cerebral vascular accident or in short an Ischemic Embolism stroke. It had blocked the blood flow to my brain arteries.. So my brain cells could not get fed the blood and oxygen they needed in order to survive. So they just died, shut down and stopped working. So the parts of my body that they were working just stopped functioning on my right side. I became completely immobile on my right side. The doctor said "I know you are not able to move your right arm, your wrist, your fingers. I know you are unable to move your right leg along with any movement of your ankle and toes". I know you are unable to speak clearly and swallow because those muscles in your throat that control those functions are very weak. In short you are completely immobile on your right side. Even though this sounds terribly bad, there is light at the end of the tunnel.

You don't have to remain like this for ever. There is something you can do", he said "There is only one thing you can do to regain the mobility of your right side and that is to stimulate other brain cells to move those body parts. You see the brain cells that were running those body parts before are dead as I said earlier. And of course again those brain cells death are not reversible. Once they're gone they're gone forever. Now you have to train other brain cells to the same job. Now you have 365 days in a year so you have a lot of time to work on them". He mentioned to me that everyone's body is not the same and that it would take some longer than others to make this happen. The fact remains it can be done on anybody. The ones who want it the most will work on it the longest. The others will hit it and get tired and give up because they don't see results right away. I remember clearly the doctor mentioned that it takes longer for some than others so don't give up. You have to push yourself if you really want it. I made up my mind when he told me it could be done. That's all I need it was to know was that I could make it happen. I didn't want any more bed pans. That was so embarrassing to me to have to go out like that. No more nurses washing me up every time I use the toilet. I didn't want to just be laid up in bed for the rest of my life. I was an athlete and I wasn't going settle for my life being cut short if I could do something about it.

After that talk my doctor gave me, it made a believer out of me right then and there. When my doctor left my bedside that morning I went to work. I started on my wrist first. Soon I could flex it up and down. All day and night I worked on it until I could move it pretty well. Once I found out how I could work that miracle on my wrist I got so exuberant and excited I worked into early morning hours. I kept comparing it to my left wrist. Man! It looked the same. So I guess I was on the right road to recovery. Soon I jumped to my fingers. One by one I started moving them with my left hand. As I saw them slowly start to move it was amazing and thrilling seeing them flex. I couldn't believe this was happening and right away I started praying when I grew tired. I knew it was the Man up above that was helping me make this possible. I continued in the wee hours of the night and into the early mornings. Next I started on my arm, bending my elbow back and forth. It was stiff, but I pushed myself even though it would hurt a little. You see when your limbs are not used for a period of time muscles and ligaments get stiff and hurt to stretch when forced. That's what was happening to me, but it didn't matter because I wanted my limbs to work. So I pushed and pulled my fingers until I got all my fingers moving and flexing along with my arm again. Once I had gotten my arm together I moved to my leg, I couldn't bend my leg, and I couldn't flex my ankle. My toes on my feet wouldn't move and flex. That really scared me out of my mind. I said to myself" I got to get my leg moving again or I won't get out of this bed". So I went to work on my leg, pulling it back and forth to get it moving with my left arm and hand trying to flex it, pushing on the railing at the foot of the bed trying to get my leg to bend and flex. It would hurt but I didn't care. I had to make this happen with my leg. I would get out of bed to squat to bend my leg and flex my toes. The nurses had the rule for me not to get out bed for fear I would fall and injure myself. But I did anyway. When they closed the door I would sneak out of the bed and work my leg. I had to do this for myself. This seemed like this was the only way I was going to get my limbs back what the therapists were doing was not working for me. I didn't want the bed pans any more. I wanted to be on my own. So every chance I got I would get out of bed to work my leg and toes. So finally one night the door was closed and I got out of bed and wouldn't you know it they caught me red handed. I was doing leg bends on the side of my bed. So the head nurse came in and scolded me. I ask her to forgive me and I wouldn't do it again. She said ok, but she went another step further and had another nurse tie me down to my bed on both legs. I couldn't believe they would do this to me. It just wasn't fair or right to tie me down to my bed even though I knew what they were doing was for my own good. This was cruel and unusual punishment for someone who had just had three strokes and was trying to pull himself together. I just couldn't fathom this kind of treatment coming from professional nurses who knew what I was trying to do for myself.

One night I was reading and I dropped my book on the floor. I didn't want to call the nurse in just to pick my book off the floor, because they would think I was just trying to get back at them for locking me down in my bed. So I untied myself from the bed on one of my legs so I could reach over the bed and pick the book up off the floor. Now the door was closed so no one could see what I was doing. As I was reaching for the book I fell completely out of bed on the floor. I tried to pull myself up and climb back into bed, but I was so weak I couldn't do it. Remember my body was already weak from the stroke on my right side. No matter how hard I tried I couldn't muster enough strength to pull myself back in bed. So I just lay there for a while hoping no one would come through that door and catch me on the floor. I knew I was in for it this time. So I tried and tried many times to pull myself back in bed, but I just didn't have the strength to manage it. After an hour of trying and trying, huffing and puffing and pulling I finally was able to get back in bed. I was so scared they were going to catch me this time. Thank God He gave me the strength to pull myself back in bed. After I got back into bed I had to just laugh at myself while trying to relax and recover after that tiring battle with the floor. That was such a dumb move to actually fall out of bed. How was I going to explain that massive move to anyone? I never told anyone before now of that incident. I was too embarrassed to relive that Kodak moment to anyone. So a couple days later I got up and went to the restroom alone without telling the nurse. I untied myself and went to relieve myself. Man it was two o'clock in the morning and I didn't want to disturb anyone at that time of morning. But I was told to call someone no matter what time it was. Wouldn't you know it? They heard me moving around and came in on me just as I stepped from my bed to enter the restroom. I thought they were going to be upset, but they just laughed and said "We got something for your butt this time". Guess what they did. The head nurse put an alarm on my bed. The alarm when set by my weight in the bed. It would go off if weight was less than what was in the bed. You know they had to go to the extremes to keep me under wraps. One day during the week they hooked the alarm up on my bed as I was reading and I dropped the book on the floor. I reached down to pick up the book off the floor. To show you how sensitive the alarm was because my weight was not evenly distributed on the bed it went off. Those nurses came running in my room looking to catch me out of bed. They came in yelling "We gotcha!" But to their surprise I was reaching out the side of my bed for the book but still in bed. I fooled them. They thought they had caught me again. We had a good laugh. So I stayed in bed all that first week under armed guard.

While in bed and what little time I spent out of bed I got my whole right side working again. I worked on myself day and night. If I wasn't sleeping or eating I was stimulating those brain cells. I was determined to get myself back together again. I worked at it with a vengeance. I made it happen for myself. By the end of the first week I had my whole right side working again before working with the therapist. Every day I spent time with a different therapist. I worked extra hard making a difference in whatever they were teaching and showing me. I would go the extra mile each session for the next week and a half. They would give me drills to perform each day and I would take them all to the extreme to master them. Nothing was too hard to perform and repeat. I did it all until I got it right and was tired. All the therapists thought I was a great student in whatever they were teaching me. Of course I wanted to go home being a whole man and not being handicapped in a wheelchair or laid up in a bed for the rest of my life. I would have the nurses walk with me around my ward several times a day learning how to walk again. It was very difficult trying to place one foot in front of the other, walking with coordination. Of course it was just like teaching a baby to walk for the first time. It took me a while to get the rhythm of putting one foot front of the other. While in therapy I would climb steps a lot each session to work my knees to the max until they hurt. I was going to get all I could out of therapist each time they saw me. I worked them all to the fullest until they were tired of me asking for more. At each of my sessions when it was over I continued to work on whatever I was doing until I got exhausted. I wanted to walk out on my own power and not be wheeled out in a chair when I went home. During my speech sessions I would spend extra time reading and saying my words aloud every day. My speech was very poor when I started. I couldn't form my words at all. It was like I hadn't ever learned to speak. When I finished my therapy I was speaking quite well so I would be understood by all who carried a conversation with me. To this day I still practice pronouncing my words and saying phrases to perfect my speaking ability. My arm movement was very slow, but progressed daily. It was difficult to move my arm certain ways. The rotation of my arm was very difficult at times, but through practice I finally got a full rotation of my arm. The therapist didn't give me exercises for my fingers. I worked on them myself. They just gave me a rubber ball to squeeze to build hand muscles. My physical therapy at North Fulton Hospital was very successful and of course much needed. Before leaving the hospital I was able to use my entire right side of my body very well. I was able to function at home with minimal assistance.

Chapter 8: Rehab Drills

Today I now work out with weights to strengthen my muscles in my hands, fingers and arms. I haven't tried to hit the heavy bag yet, which I used to do often when I was boxing, but the speed bag I can hit ok when I concentrate. When it came to my legs I tried to run on the tread mill for about five to ten minutes after coming home and going to the gym. That went alright for that short period of time. My right leg wouldn't keep up if I went too fast. After coming home I tried to run in the backyard. To my disappointment my right leg would not keep up with my left leg at all. I would just drag it along. I could not pick it up and move it in coordination with my left leg no matter what I did to try and keep up the pace. I hadn't tried to run on the track yet. I was scared of falling on the track if I tired. I hadn't tried running stairs yet either. My legs seemed pretty strong so I wanted to test my knees on bleacher stairs really soon. The therapist gave me exercises for my whole hand not just my fingers with a rubber ball. So I got my fingers working by stimulating those brain cells and practicing touching each one of them to my thumb. I used the jacks and the pick-up sticks when I went home from the hospital. I used them every day for my finger therapy. They made a big difference in the use of my hand in holding things and gripping objects with it. While in the hospital I worked on my speech every day for an hour mastering word pronunciation and phrases. For my arm I was taken through a list of arm and hand exercises to fully

102

use them both regularly for everyday use. This was done at least an hour a day also without fail. Then some portion of the day for an hour I would get some great therapy for daily occupational management. I was still learning how to brush my teeth. I couldn't hold my toothbrush. I was still trying to teach myself how to shave without cutting myself. Putting on my clothes was a big chore for me also as well as buttoning my shirt and zipping up my pants. I had a hard time learning how to tie my shoes again. I had such a difficult time holding my eating utensils and feeding myself too. I kept dropping my food just before I got it to my mouth right in my lap. That took me a long time to master. That was so frustrating for me. I would be so hungry, but I couldn't get any food to my mouth with my right hand. So I would use my left hand until I got full and I then would use my right hand to practice getting the food to my mouth. I had to also use a utensil holder for about a week that fit around the handle of a spoon, fork and knife so I could grip them to handle them with comfort without dropping them. Once I was able to form the finger positions to use them with ease and comfort I stopped using the utensil holder. I tell you it was just like teaching an infant to feed themselves. I was so clumsy with my right hand I thought I wasn't ever going to get it together at all, but I stayed with the program until I got it. Man! That was such a relief to be able to eat without help. That was a major step for me in getting back into the main stream of life for me.

Thus, every day was a new adventure for me working with the different types of therapists trying to revitalize my whole right side from head to toe. The therapy sessions with the physical therapist, speech therapist, and occupational therapist were all grueling sessions to say the least. They made me work at everything they put me through to the max. If I wanted to rest they would take me to another level. So I stopped saying I was tired. It was for my own good though. I had told them from the very beginning to push me to the limit in every exercise. That's what they did from the beginning to the end of each session with me. They did not let up even if I complained my muscles were hurting and tired. I am certainly glad they were willing to assist me like I had asked. I don't believe they were normally this rough with most patients. I asked for what they gave me. They didn't want to drive me as hard as I asked, but I had them make me work so I would be prepared for the world at home. So they put it on me. Every day I was ready for what the therapist planned for me. You know sometimes you have to be careful of what you ask for because you might get it and you might certainly regret that you ask. In this case I wanted and needed just what they gave me. Every day I was getting better at using my arm with the functioning of my fingers and hand. With my walking I was slowly putting one foot in front of the other using my arms swinging to help me balance myself. It all seemed so new to me even though I had been using them all my life. It was just so strange to have to teach myself the art of walking again and how to use my arms to balance myself. I had to practice that form of walking so many times to get it right so I could walk straight. They had a gait belt to keep you from falling while learning how to walk. This belt goes around your waist with about two-foot extension for someone to hold to keep you from falling to the ground or bumping up against walls or objects while waking. It's similar to a child's harness used by parents to keep their children from running off out in public. It is very beneficial for learning how to walk again as a stroke victim. It was a great tool for me. I didn't feel embarrassed using it either, because whatever it took to get me back on my feet again I would do. So I would use this tool every day with the therapist walking up and down the halls of my ward. My balance was terrible starting off. Of course as I grew used to being on my feet it got easier. I tell you it was scary learning how to walk again. The fear of falling to the ground was on my mind every step I took. I heard so many times about seniors falling and breaking their hips. I certainly didn't want that, because the healing process was so long if they healed at all. I certainly didn't want that to deal with at this time of my life. So I took all precautions necessary to be safe.

Once I had walking down I could concentrate on other things in the occupational management area like shaving, buttoning up my shirts, tying my shoes, and zipping up my pants. I never guessed that tying my shoes would be so challenging, though it was. It was difficult to get my fingers to work the right way in folding over the strings to make a bow. I was getting frustrated at repeatedly tying of the bow over and over again. Finally I got the hang of it. It was a bitter experience. I thought I would never get it right. I was so happy that was over with. The buttoning of my shirt was trying also. I couldn't get my fingers to roll, sliding the buttons in the holes of my shirt. The top button of my shirt was the most difficult to orchestrate to get the button into the hole. My arms and my fingers both grew so tired trying to get the button to stay in the holes of the shirt. The next feat was brushing my teeth. It was so hard to get the up and down movement of brush on my teeth and not my lips. I kept missing my mouth. I kept hitting my cheeks and my chin. Once I got the brush in my mouth I had difficulty with the up and down movement. It was like slow motion. I just couldn't get the brush to move quickly up and down at all. It took some time to get that coordination down so I could get my teeth brushed in a reasonable good time. I finally accomplished it in just a few minutes. My physical therapist spent a lot of time teaching me to print and write again. That was really tough to learn to print my letters again. I couldn't remember the correct way to form the letters of the alphabet. I just couldn't remember the way to make them on the page of lined paper. It was something not to be able to print the letters of the alphabet on line paper correctly. We forget as we get older and not have to do it at any time. As a child I did learn how to print, but not well because I didn't practice. I remember as a child I didn't like to print at all. So I never developed any good printing skills. The same way with my writing skills. I did learn how to write correctly, but I never practiced at all. So here I had another chance to learn again. The therapist didn't spend a lot of time on either one. They made sure I could do both with some accuracy and clarity so it could be read and understood. It was up to me to practice if I wanted to improve either. I did practice them both to make some vast improvements. So I think my writing is better, but my printing is still poor even though you can make out my letters. For two and a half weeks I learned the basics on speaking, forming my letters with my mouth and reading aloud to the therapist. For my arm and fingers I was given exercises to stretch my fingers and the muscles in my hand and of course I had stimulated brain cells to get the process moving. Exercises to work the rotation of the arm were also put into play to get the complete movement of the arm left and right. This also included learning all things necessary to take care of myself in the morning after waking up from putting on my clothes to going to the bathroom. At the end of two and a half weeks, I was ready to go home and face the world without a handicap. I was ready to go home and get back into the real world.

Chapter 9: Going Home

I was ready to go home. It was 3-11-11 and the hospital was getting me ready to go home on 3-12-11. So I had to decide where I was going when I left the hospital. Well I had to go where I would be cared for 24/7 until I could go home and take care of myself. Well Ms. C could not take care of me, because she was working in the evening. So Ms. V was called to see if she would take care of me 24/7, and fortunately she said yes she could. That's where I was hoping I could go to recover. I was so in love with Ms. V and of course she was so much in love with me also I believed. Ms. V was given authorization by North Fulton Hospital to come get me after I was discharged. Now keep in mind she didn't have to do it, but because we were so into each other she opened up her home to me to make me comfortable. Keep in mind that we had never lived together during the course of our relationship. We only would visit each other from time to time, but we never stayed at each other's home longer than overnight. So we didn't know how it would be being under each other every day.

So March 12, 2011 began our living together. She was a very gracious host to say the least. She made me very comfortable and secure. She was there for all of my needs. She was in the beginning the perfect caregiver and women to me. She was not use to cooking for anyone but herself and that was one of the biggest hurdles she had to face. She hadn't cooked for anyone since her children left home. Now her two kids were in their thirties. There were many things she couldn't cook. Now keep in mind I was not a great cook either. So it was almost like the blind leading the blind. I had always cooked for myself and so had she. Since I had been with Ms. C for a while I had learned some things about how to cook some meals. Ms. C was a great cook to say the least. She could get down with any meal. So I picked upon some things from Ms. C and passed on the information to Ms. V hoping she would recreate some meals. Now this was very difficult to do mind you. Ms. V didn't like to be told how to do things especially in her kitchen. It was very delicate to get her to follow some of my directions in cooking. If I was sharing some ingredients for a recipe and she didn't agree she would get upset and stop cooking. She wanted to make whatever she was cooking herself without any help. If I had something I wanted cooked a certain way and not her way she would get real upset and ask me to cook it myself. So If I wanted a certain meal cooked it would have to be cooked her way or I wouldn't get it. It was her way or the highway with cooking. I could not be in the kitchen when my meals were cooked. This would go for breakfast too. She would let me know that she was capable of making what I wanted to eat. After a few weeks it got where she was doing pretty good with my meals.

Going to therapy two to three times a week got old real soon too. We had to travel out to Douglasville two to three times a week. She didn't like putting the miles on her car. Ms. V didn't like to drive me everywhere I needed to go. She just hated driving. She would complain about the wear and tear on her car. Also I had to start going to my Real Estate Classes twice a week out in Morrow, Georgia. She didn't like that at all. It was fortunate that Ms. V's daughter was attending classes in Real Estate at the same location and time, so I was able to go with her daughter for my classes. That worked out nicely for the duration of the classes.

My therapy at home while staying with Ms. V was great. I had a bathroom to myself where I didn't have to rush at any time of the day. If I needed help with anything

Ms. V was there to assist me with whatever I needed. I had a pulley to stretch my arm muscles on my right side. There was the ball and jacks I used to build my dexterity of my fingers and hand. I also used rice and beans I would throw on the carpet and then pick them up one piece at a time. I had a pack of Pick UP Sticks I also used for my hand and finger dexterity. Ms. V's daughter also gave me some books to help me with my handwriting and printing skills. I worked on my dexterity with some wooden blocks Ms. V's daughter gave me too. Ms. V and her daughter were very instrumental in getting my arm, hand, and leg on my right side working normal again without a doubt. They pushed me to the max and made me work them all the time while I was with Ms. V.

For my physical therapy for my right leg I did a lot of walking every day around several blocks in the neighborhood. The streets which I took walks had steep hills to challenge my leg strength and my balance. There were stairs also in the home in which I climbed several times a day up and down. For my hand and finger strength I did pushups several times a day on the carpet in the house.

I also started going to the gym and working out with the weights about three months after getting home from the hospital. Also I swam once a week about 1200 meters for about an hour. So I was getting my muscle building and my cardio work out each week. Ms. V would always make sure I went to the gym and pool on the days that I regularly went and made sure I got my exercise in. I'd tried to get Ms. V to go swimming with me, but the chlorine made her ill, so I never pushed going swimming with me. We did walk together around the neighborhood once or twice a week. We would use this time to talk about things that would be on our minds that we never talked about at dinner or just sitting around the house. For some reason the walks would be better to air out our problems. I guess that's why we were so true to each other. If we had something on either of our minds we could get it out when we were alone at some time. We never kept things bottled up inside. We both knew it wasn't healthy for the relationship so we always said what was on our minds to clear the air. We tried to go different places as often as we could to keep the relationship fresh. We would go dancing, live jazz, go to the park and have picnics. Sometimes we went out to the lake and watched the boats go by with our feet in the water while eating junk food. We would take trips to Savanna Georgia, Tybee Island, and Hilton Head also near Savanna. We also would go to places like Macon,

Georgia to the Georgia Music Hall of Fame. So we did a variety of outings all the time to keep it fresh and alive. Now there were times we got tired of each other and Ms. V would ask me to leave. She knew I had someone who could step in and take over the reins if she didn't treat me right. Often we would get into heated verbal confrontations and I would have her take me home. Now we loved each other madly we just needed our space for a while, so in haste she would pack my things and throw it in the car and take me home. We didn't know how to defuse the confrontations so this happened each time she took me home. Once I got home I would call Ms. C and let her know where I was and she would come over and pick me up. This went on for at least four months' time after I had been discharged from the hospital. I would stay with Ms. C for a while until I would make up with Ms. V. I would then ask Ms. C to take me home and immediately when I got home I would call Ms. V to come and pick me up from my house and take me back to her place. I would be so happy to see Ms. V and of course she was very happy to see me too. This same thing went on for at least four more times exactly the same way. We just could not stay away from each other. So finally Ms. V had enough and decided not to see me anymore. By the fourth time this occurred I was able to take care of myself, but I still couldn't do anything in the kitchen. I couldn't handle the pots and pans. My dexterity with hot pots and pans was just not safe. I would drop them when trying to handle them so I still needed someone to help me to take of myself. I just needed someone to cook for me. So I was able to get Ms. C to cook for me. She was the most qualified for the task. Ms. C would cook all my meals and bring them to my home. She would do breakfast and dinner. She and I made a deal that I would pay her every two weeks for preparing my meals each week. There isn't anything in the kitchen that Ms. C can't do or make. She is a wonderful woman in the kitchen. She is one of the best. She went to culinary school and learned from some of the best chefs in Atlanta, so I had one of the best cooks working with me while trying to recover.

As I was still unable to drive, I had Ms. C to take me everywhere I needed to go and I would buy the gas for the car. She would take me to therapy visits every week at least two times in Douglasville. When I would go to the gym three times a week to work out and my swimming once or twice a week, she was very nice about all the driving she would have to do for me. As a matter of fact she encouraged me to go to the gym and also to swim. She would stay on me about using my tools for home therapy. She really did push me a lot. Of course when we would go on outings she would drive there also. We would go to places like Savanna, Tybee Island, Hilton Head and some of the lakes here in Georgia. We went to where President Carter was from and visited the exhibits on his life and his President term in office. We went to the Cherry Blossom Festival in Macon Georgia and the Georgia Music Hall of Fame. We would go to places like Selma, Montgomery, Alabama, Virginia and Washington DC. We had such great times. One thing about Ms. C she did not ever complain about driving ever. She wanted to drive and enjoyed it. I was so happy about that because I did not want to drive ever again. As a passenger you see a lot potential accidents that the driver just doesn't see and some unpreventable things. I found it frightening being a passenger, though she turned out to be a pretty good driver. I trust her with my life as a passenger, so not being able to drive has its advantages. I could always look forward to a nice comfortable ride. I was relaxed and worried free of anything around us, just enjoying the ride and the view from the shotgun side of the car. Having Ms C as my personal driver had its draw backs though, like leaving on time to be somewhere on time for some function. Being picked up on time and not having to

116

wait at night or being picked up on a cold day while waiting outside. This was the killer. You have a craving for something and no one is around to take you to get it. You call, but you can't get anyone by text or by cell phone. So what do you do? You just be patient and wait until you can get your driver to take you. That's all you can do for now. To make this work better for me I would stay with Ms. C so she would not have to bring my meals to me every morning and every night for dinner. What she would do is take me home once or twice a week to check on things and take me back home with her. This same arrangement was used with Ms. V when I was staying with her. It was like pulling teeth of course to get her to take me to check on things once or twice a week at home. Of course the distance was much shorter with Ms. C, because she lived about seven minutes from my home.

While I stayed with Ms. C she really encouraged me to spend a lot time on my therapy. She had me work on everything every day of the week without fail, so I could get stronger and more efficient to do and handle everyday things that I would encounter on a daily basis. By then the only things I couldn't do for myself were cook and drive. I tried to cook, but I could not hold the pots and pans in my hands whether they were hot or not. I kept dropping them on the floor. I kept dropping glasses of liquid I would have in my hands on the floor. I am to this day still trying to teach my right hand how to let things go after I grip them in my hand and want to release them. It's getting better every day. Fall 2011 marked my last speech therapy session. My speech skills are still little weak. All in all I'm real proud of myself of what I pulled together to become somewhat self-sufficient.

Going back and forth from Ms. V to Ms. C's during the first year of my stroke they have both noticed and commended me on how well I had caught up with life since my stroke. They both thought I was still able to compete in the game of life though I was assisted with a cane. In January 2012 after Ms. C.'s mother had passed, I stayed at Ms. C's house all the time. She would take me home from time to time to piddle around just to keep busy at times. Secretly Ms. V and I would contact each other after the misunderstanding had cooled down. This went on for months that we would see each other when Ms. C would take me to the gym to work out and swim twice a week. When Ms. C. would drop me off at the gym I would call Ms. V to pick me up. This went on for months at a time.

Finally Ms. C got wise to what I was doing and caught me red handed when Ms. V was dropping me off back at the gym after we had visited one sunny afternoon. Man was I surprised when Ms. C walked up behind me just after I was dropped off by Ms. V. and touched me on my shoulder. Bam!! I was busted. All I could do was smile. Of course that ended that pick-up and drop-off. So I had to see Ms. V less often. I just had Ms. V visit me at my house once or twice a week when Ms. C would take me home to busy myself. Both of those women were so much a part of my life I couldn't give either one of them up. They both did everything they could to assist me in my rehabilitation from my stroke. They both were very supportive of me that you would have thought I was married to them both. Their families also supported me in my recovery. I had the best of all three worlds my family, Ms. V's crew and the family of Ms. C all rooting for my getting well soon. I was working very hard to make large strides in getting all of my limbs strong and functional again. So every week I was hitting the gym and pool trying to make it happen.

It was around March 25, 2013 I was trying to walk without a cane. I would get wobbly at times and a little dizzy while walking without the cane. I would hit walls or fixed objects to support myself to walk straight, though I kept going. I would lose my balance and get some what disoriented, but I seemed to get through it. I went to the gym and braved through it the first time out without my cane. I moved slowly and methodically through my workout. Everyone noticed right away when I walked in the gym and congratulated me on my efforts trying to push myself. This was true when I returned to the gym and started swimming again also. People were amazed at how I just seemed to pull it all together from memory and make it happen. I believe it's a gift from God along with being an athlete all those years. As a professional athlete I have always pushed myself to the limits.

I have always been a daredevil of some sorts all my life. Point in case recently on April 16, 2013 at about midnight I was staying home one evening. Miss C had brought me home. I was watching movies on my HBO movie station that night. I was getting hungry for some snacks like ice cream, popcorn and soda. Man I had the real munches. I was craving some popcorn but there wasn't any in the house. I tried to get it out of my mind. I would start watching the movies and immediately I started tasting popcorn. No matter what I did I just couldn't get it out of my mind. It was about midnight and my car was sitting waiting for me. I knew I could barely walk and now I wanted to drive to the store and get some junk food. I said to myself, "Man you are out of your mind. You can't drive a car. You know you can't judge the distance when turning and stopping". So I just let that thought go. It kept haunting me when I started watching the movies. Over and over again it kept flexing in my head. So finally I thought about it real hard. So I said to myself trying to convince me to do it, "Man, I'm going. It's midnight and not too many people are on the road. The Kroger is close by. I can make it." So I took a deep breath and said "I'm going to try it". I got my keys and went down to the garage. I looked at my Camaro looking at me, saying "Come on Rock lets go." So I said "What the hell? I'm going." I opened the car door and looked in and said no. My stomach started crawling for that popcorn and soda. I jumped in and turned the key before I could talk myself out of it again. I pulled the car carefully out of the garage and straightened it out to drive out the driveway. I eased the car to the edge of the driveway by the street. I looked both ways; there was no one coming so I eased out into street. I pushed the accelerator to 20mph then 25mph to get to the end of the street. Now I was at the main drag waiting to turn right. I looked both ways and no one was coming. So I eased out on to the street and cleared the curve for my right turn. I was on my way, but a little scared. Still there were no other cars but mine. That was good. No competition. So I moved on down the street at 20 mph. I then got to the big main street South Cobb Drive. I came to a smooth stop and looked both ways. There was only one car on the main street. I had to make a right turn. I was trying to make it wide enough to clear the curve. Wouldn't you know it I didn't? I ran all over the curve and bounced down back on to the street. I'm glad no one saw me make that right turn. So after I straightened up the car and got on my way I was good. The store was not far after the right turn thank God. When I reached the store, I pulled into the parking lot and eased on to the area where the parking was. I found a close parking space and got in it quickly. I was so glad to reach the store in one piece. So I got my popcorn and returned home very slowly around 20 mph. I tell you I was really afraid on the road even though there wasn't anybody on the road but me. What I hated most was making right and left turns. To this day that's the most difficult thing to do while driving. I made it back home and enjoyed my popcorn and soda with ice cream. I'm glad I stepped out on faith and tried it. It goes to show you that you can do a lot of things that you might be afraid of if you just step out on faith. I don't think I would be where I am today if I had not pushed myself out on faith. I just made up my mind I could do it. Because I had not been able to handle things in my hands and not being able to judge distances along with my eye hand coordination I doubted myself. My friends and neighbors were telling me I could do it too. I really was tired of depending on others to take me here and there too. I'm glad I pulled the strings loose. I knew Mrs. C was getting tired of taking me places too. I wanted to help her but I was too afraid to try. I had seen so many things that caused accidents as a passenger I just didn't want to get back out there. When I drove to the gym everyone was so surprised they couldn't believe it. They all congratulated me and cheered me on. Now I had gained another part of my independence—to move around freely when I wanted to.

Chapter 10: Water Sporting Interest

This just came to my mind about pushing myself in unknown territory. There were always things I wanted to do as a kid. There was something as a kid growing up living in the Black Ghetto in South Central Los Angeles I wanted so much to do. I couldn't tell my friends about it because it was something only white kids did and that was surf. Oh man I really enjoyed watching the white kids surf. My parents would take our family to the beaches in Los Angeles, Long Beach, Venice, Manhattan, El Segundo, Santa Monica, Malibu and San Pedro and I would watch the guys surf. I knew I could do it but I certainly couldn't let any of my friends know I was even thinking about it. If I had I would have been labeled a nerd and an outcast. So I just kept it to myself.

Our family moved into a well-kept Black neighborhood in southwestern Los Angeles when I was in ninth grade in 1962. We had lived with Aunt Estelle for about a year. It was a nice move from South Central Los Angeles. The area was much, much nicer. It was like night and day. The schools and people were very different. The people in the neighborhood were mindful of their property and area in which they lived. Everyone kept their home well-manicured. All the neighbors had a lot of pride in their own home. It was a nice thing to see nice Black homes. It was a good experience for the whole family as we experienced new things. However, we adjusted real easily as we all wanted better things for the whole family and this was our opportunity. Then about year later my parents bought their own home in an all-white neighborhood. I attended Verbum Dei High School in Watts California for one year. The students who went to Verbum Dei were all from different areas of Los Angeles and were all Black or Latino. We had problems on the bus stops going to school in Watts. The kids in the area who lived in Watts would try and take our money while we waited for bus every day. You had to be tough in order to fight off the bad elements with any success. If you didn't know how to fight you learned quickly if you wanted to survive. As a small kid I learned to defend myself so I had always been in good shape even in the ninth grade. After the first year at Verbum Dei I transferred to an all-White Catholic Boys High School called Serra High in Gardena, California. Here is where my dream of surfing became a reality. That year my classmates took me along with them to the local beaches to surf. Man I thought I was in surf heaven. I learned to do something I only read about and saw from a distance or on television. I would go as often as I could. I even bought myself a surf board. All my classmates had their own boards. So I had to get one too so I could be a part of the gang.

I had a great time in tenth grade. That's when I was a Black surfer. I was pretty darn good too. My girl cousins who were in high school would make fun of me all the time, but that didn't bother me. What did they know? See they went to an all-Black high school in the inner-city and there was no surfing there. I did just what I wanted to do no matter what people said. I enjoyed myself. I had a great time with my White friends at Serra. Even then I was in great shape physically. You had to be to handle those boards in those days. Those boards were eight feet long and heavy too. You couldn't be a weakling and surf. You had to be a good swimmer and strong enough to handle the board itself too. The water was always cold so in the months not in summer you had to have a wet suit like skin divers use.

Scuba diving was very popular then too. I didn't learn or have an interest in scuba diving until I came to

Georgia in 1985. Even though I had been around scuba diving all my life in the Los Angeles area I never had an interest at all. I did get my PADI Cert to dive in a class at Georgia State University in 1986. I got my PADI Cert in Panama City Florida in 1986. Also I learn to sail. I would also go on sailing trips every weekend for about two years straight. We went to Panama City (my wife then and me) and rented a catamaran after we both took the class at GSU and sailed for two days. Man we had a ball. The weather was just beautiful that weekend. I also learned to waterski. I became so good I was able to slalom ski, which means skiing on one ski. I was so good when we would go out on a ski trip I would always be the best skier and the only Black one too. I was always pretty good at everything I did in sports. I always kept myself in great shape. I was able to do these things because I pushed myself, and stepped out on faith that I could make it happen. So I pushed myself to overcome my stroke disabilities too in the same way.

Chapter 11: Looking Back

April 21, 2014 marked three years two months since my stroke. In 2013, I thought I knew what I was going to do for some time to come. I put together a presentation on strokes after I had done some research. The presentation consisted of information on what a stroke was, how it was formed, and the four most common types of strokes: Ischemic, Embolism, Thrombosis, Hemorrhagic. I then listed the statistics involving strokes, explaining how and why depression sets in stroke patients. From there I explained the attending physician's role with the stroke patient. I then moved on to the taking of medication and the transition into rehabilitation which should start immediately if not sooner. Then I had a fifteen-minute question and answer period. The entire presentation was an hour and a half. I would travel throughout Atlanta presenting to several senior centers and senior apartment homes. My presentations seemed to have been well received and needed. I made eight presentations in all. After my eighth showing there seemed to be no interest in what I was giving back to the community. I would videotape most of my outings so I would have something to show others who wanted know what my presentations were all about and of course for my own records. My fifth outing was my largest of all with 162 people in the audience. This one was at the center where Ms. V worked part-time. She assisted me in obtaining this venue to give my presentation. I had such a great response I couldn't sit down after I gave my presentation. All the people who came up to me mentioned how I had touched them in some way with something I said. I have to say that was one of my greatest moments as a speaker. I thought at that time this was my calling. But I think not. I believe my work as a speaker has been fulfilled after my worst outing on November 19, 2013. Nothing went right even though I was on time with all my set up. I was asked to go on late and to top that off they wouldn't allow me to do my entire presentation. I was very upset but I didn't let on to anyone that I very angry. I handled it like a professional and I just packed my things and left quietly. I don't think anyone noticed that I was gone. I was so embarrassed and angry because I would start my presentation and then be stopped and say something else that was out of context. The program narrator stopped me several times into my presentation. I lost my place several times because of that stopping and starting. So finally I just ended it and got off stage. Nobody even apologized to me for the interruptions. I didn't complain; I just got off stage nicely with a smile. That was my last outing. I believe I did what all I was supposed to do with my gift of life by giving back what was given to me through my presentation. The purpose of my presentation was to share with others how to recover after having a stroke. Most stroke victims either die or don't ever recover. It was a miracle I recovered, because I was given the knowledge to be able to make it happen. Thank God for my doctor who gave me the message.

Here and now I have continued to work on myself physically and mentally to restore my self-worth. I still go to the gym at least three times a week to work on my body and swim once a week to manage my cardiology functions. I watch sports on television like boxing, football, track, basketball and wish I could have my ability and age back to compete once more. You look at yourself in the mirror and wonder what it would be like if you could do all again. What would be the outcome? Would you be a better athlete or would it be the same? You wonder if you gave it your best. Did you? I wonder looking back on my last two professional fights. There were things I would have done differently. Why didn't I at the time? Did I know what to do or did I not have the right advice? Was I indeed in shape to perform? I thought I was. Why did I make the decisions that I made at that time? I know I didn't at the time have a manager to coach me through the rounds. I couldn't see what a trainer would see if there was one present. I knew in both of my last fights I was in great shape. What I didn't have was someone to guide me through the rounds. It was like now when Ms. Y would drive me around and I would see all the potential accidents waiting to happen. In my matches my corner would have seen things I of course didn't and couldn't see because I was driving in the fights. If there was some way I could do it all again I know I would do it differently. God I wish there were some way. You know I was really good. I'm not just saying it. I really was. God I wish I could do it again. Oh well! So much for making right decision when needed. I look at myself and say what do I do now for excitement and competition? What's left that I can do? I think about what I'd like to do with my life now, like venture into education and study forensics, uncovering data at crime scenes with science probes and instruments. I need something of this fashion to keep me moving and targeted on life now that I am retired with time on my hands.

In May 2014 I was living back at home with my own transportation to come and go as I pleased. I went to the gym three times a week and swam once a week. I felt I needed more to complete my life as it was now. Education seemed the way I should go to challenge myself in the twilight of my life. My health seemed to be intact since I had my strokes and taking meds to smooth out my medical issues. I still have one handicap in that I can't cook for myself. I fortunately have Ms. Y to assist me in this gray area of my life as it is. Soon I will be able to do more for myself as far as preparing my meals again. My working out and swimming has helped me so much I'm almost back to normal. I've still yet to challenge my body in contact sports yet or running on the track. I want to try tennis or basketball to see how I hold out with others bumping me and pushing me around while running. I think I can do it without any big problems I hope. I'm also going to try to hit the speed bag and see if I can get in a rhythm with my arms, legs and hands. I'm also going to see if I can run on the tract a few times to see if my cardio is still there. It's been three years three months since my three strokes. I need to see where I am physically. I'm really excited to know what I can do. I do believe my former physical condition has set the pace for me to come back strong and be what I was. We shall see soon. Looking back on what has happened to me since February 15, 2011 the day of my first stroke, I know if I hadn't been into athletics all these years of my life at this time I would be laying in a bed or sitting in a wheelchair staring at the world going by. Even worse dead and buried six feet under. Being fit body, mind and soul all your life along with knowing the secret of stimulating other brain cells in defeating the killer called stroke is key. All those things you heard about all your life to keep fit and active were all so true.

Once you stop being active your body and mind start to have withdrawal symptoms which you may not recognize. Soon your body starts to deteriorate without your realizing it. Pretty soon you become weak and sick for no rhyme or reason. The body is a strange and wonderful organ that has a being all its own. It reacts and marches to its own drum beat. Everyone has his or her own beat to their body that's unique to that individual. It's only for that person body and that person body knows it. When something in that person's body is not in tune, that body reacts negatively. That's when you start feeling and looking rundown. So activeness is a must with our shells of a body. You have to keep it active or it will slow down and die.

Now that I am sixty-five my body wants to slow down and quit working. I won't let it because there's so much I still want to do and see. I keep oiling it so it will continue to work for me. It's a constant effort and push to keep it running smoothly. Besides I'm a fighter when it comes to my health and faith. When it comes to your health and faith you have to be committed to making it work for you. Only you can make a difference in your life. Just you and no one else. When you are born you have help, but when you die you die alone. Your longevity depends on you taking care of yourself in your younger years for the most parts. The building blocks you set in place as a youth supports what you do in the future. Your health is for the most part what it is to be in your later years is dictated by how you have taken care of yourself in your youth and in your young adult years. If you have done well with your diet and you have exercised on a regular basis throughout your life as a senior your health will stand the test of time because of how have treated yourself. When different ailments arrive during your senior years you will be able to fight them with a vengeance because you have set a good foundation during your younger years. Just like a car or anything mechanical working thing, if you have done regular maintenance on it throughout its life it will run smoothly longer than its life

134

expectancy. The human body is the same way. You keep it oiled and well maintained it will last longer than its life expectancy. I truly believe that is why I was able to survive those strokes along with the grace of God not wanting me to come home just yet. I am so adamant about taking care of one 's self. It's the cornerstone of life's longevity of one's body. This has been instilled in me ever since I learned what an athlete was at the age of five or six.

For those who read my book if you don't get anything from the reading I want you to get this point. Without your health you have nothing. Nothing you may have doesn't mean anything if you don't have your health so you can't enjoy it. With your health you have everything. You can enjoy anything you may have whether you are broke or well off financially. If you should lose what you have you can get some more. Your health once it's gone is no more. You can't buy your health back. Once it goes you will never be the same whole person ever again. Have yourself and others in your family checked out at least once a year by your family physician. Make it part of your life style and live. Stay healthy and live long.

Acknowledgements

I would like to thank God for the writing of this book my Lord and Savior, who by His mercy and grace gave me another chance at life surrounded by a cast of many. The chosen few that were sent by God Almighty to assist me in surviving my strokes are as follows. The man that delivered the miracle of healing was my physician Dr. Harbin. He explained to me in detail what I had to do to regain the use of my limbs by stimulating other brain cells. The brain cells that moved my right side of my body before I had my stroke had died during my strokes so other brain cells had to be charged and stimulated.

As it happened I had no one to care for me when I was released from North Fulton Hospital for rehabilitation. A very gracious giving and willing lady Ms. Vivian Talley stepped up to the plate and opened up her home to me to channel me on my way to recovery. She and her daughter La Tonya Avery and her family just went the extra mile to make me feel welcome and comfortable. Ms. Talley made sure all my meals were met and that I had transportation to all my appointments for doctors and therapy sessions. Ms. Talley and her daughter Mrs. Avery were also gracious to make a way for me to get my Real Estate classes following my released from the hospital. They both along with their family were crucial to my start of my initial recovery back to the world.

I would not be as far along with my recovery today if Ms. Yolanda Celik had not been there for me providing me with transportation and preparing my meals. She was very instrumental in getting me to doctor appointments and therapy sessions until I was able to drive myself as of April of 2013. Now still to this day Ms. Celik is graciously helping me from time to time to get my meals because I am unable to perform some cooking task in the kitchen.

I certainly want to acknowledge the doctors and nurses as well as the sitting staff that cared for me 24/7 at Northside Hospital during my stay. They all were so gracious and giving of their services for the entire time of my stay. They set the ground work for my recovery for what was to come.

The staff at North Fulton Hospital was so professional and tuned to my specific needs of recovery. The nurses and the therapist who attended to all my needs as well as the wonderful Dr. Harbin who went beyond the call of duty: I owe them all much. Because of them I was sent home with a whole new lease on life that I wouldn't have had otherwise.

"A gracious receiver never disappoints a giver."

Donald S. Herring (Rock)

February 2013, Smyrna, Georgia

Made in the USA
Columbia, SC
27 April 2022